The Cursed Coin

Check out the other books in the

FRIGHTVISION

series:

Picture Day

Wishful Thinking

Framed for Life

#GraveyardChallenge

FRIGHTVISION

The Cursed Coin

Culliver Crantz

Cover illustration: Brett Kelley
Cover Design: Stephanie Gaston

www.FrightVisionBooks.com

Facebook: @FrightVisionBooks

**J
FRIGHTVISION**

Dearest Visitor,

Welcome!

What you're about to experience isn't real ... but it could be. Who's to say?

You'll see and imagine things that you might enjoy or that could cause you fright. Don't panic. It's worse if you do.

Perhaps these are all just nightmares anyway, but only time will tell.

Sweetest Dreams,

Crantz

CHAPTER ONE

"Come on, Shelly. Hurry up!" I yelled to my younger sister, who was dragging behind on our walk around the neighborhood. Darkness was taking over the summer evening sky.

"Wait a sec, I found something cool." Shelly bent down, her dark jeans touching the warm pavement. She had a brown stain on her left knee. It looked like she'd stuck her leg in a muddy swamp. But Shelly didn't care. She was never afraid to get dirty.

My ten-year-old sister looked like a mouse but acted like a bear. She was short and skinny. Both of her legs together were the width of one of mine. She also had long, blonde hair and blue eyes, much different than my short, dark hair and brown eyes. I was two years older than

Shelly and a little husky—bear-like, but I hardly acted like one.

"Check this out, RJ," she called to me.

My eyes rolled as she examined something shiny on the ground. Every time we went anywhere, Shelly tried to bring something home with her. The scarier the better—like the pet spider we had for two weeks, the snapping turtle that nearly bit my finger off, or the rock that looked like a skull. I *hated* scary things, which was why I was always skeptical about seeing whatever she found.

I reached for the yellow bucket hat that was draped around my neck. It had been my dad's. The black cord attached to it allowed me to let it hang from my neck when I didn't want it on my head. I pulled the cap to my head and tugged down on the brim so that my eyes were covered.

"RJ, lift up your hat and come look at this," Shelly said. "There's nothing to be scared of."

Nervously, I turned my head, doing my best to pretend I couldn't hear her. Too bad it didn't stop her from continuing to yell my name.

"You know I hate this spot. One of these times you're going to get us in trouble over here." My body tensed up. A rush of panic and fear attacked my chest. I knew it was silly. We were in our neighborhood, but I couldn't stop my reactions.

"Oh, come on. Relax a little, would ya?" Shelly remained crouched over her find.

I didn't need to see what it was. I was already on edge as we were approaching the two leafless trees of the cul-de-sac at the end of our block. This was where we were supposed to turn back. Not far behind those trees was an old, eerie castle-like house—number thirteen. And behind it, the lake that changed my life forever.

Chills swarmed my body. The house stood vacant. Moss and scraggly vines crawled across the foundation, which looked like it might fall over at any moment. But at one time, the house must have been amazing. It was massive, more than three times the size of any of the other houses in the neighborhood and it looked like a castle.

A locked, rusted gate hid the driveway entrance. When the wind blew, it creaked like an old teeter totter, knocking against the No Trespassing sign. The fence connected to the gate was only a few feet high and missing pieces as parts had collapsed over the years. Shards of glass, water bottles, empty candy wrappers, and plastic bags littered the yard, releasing a nasty odor. Given how bad it smelled, I wouldn't be surprised to find something dead in the tall grass.

Behind the house was a steep slope that led to a cliff towering over a large lake, which I could barely see. The view from the backyard of the castle's house must be incredible, but because of what happened to my dad, I never wanted to go near that lake. It seemed that everything that disappeared into that water, never came back.

The hairs on the back of my neck shot to life as we neared the old house. I paced back and forth, waiting for my sister to figure out if she should keep whatever she had found. I hated when she got sidetracked on our walks.

Each time we made it all the way to the cul-de-sac, I wondered if Shelly would run onto the lawn of the abandoned house and dare me to join her. That was one of my many fears. Add that to heights, spiders, snakes, weird noises, dying, ghosts, and so on. I couldn't help it. I didn't know how not be afraid of those things. My dad never had the opportunity to show me how to be brave like him. He wasn't scared of anything. Still, hopefully, one of these days I'll be more normal—at least that's what Ed says.

Ed is Mom's new boyfriend. If you ask me, he's a little off. Sure, he's smart and kinda nerdy like me, being a scientist and all he has to be. But he cares way too much about how scared I am. Why won't he let me be? It seems he either wants me to not be afraid of anything or find out what I'm scared of and torture me. It's so irritating.

"Check this out!" Shelly called again.

Flying fishsticks. Reluctantly, I walked toward her, knowing that was the only way I was going to get her to go home. I didn't like being out late at night, wandering around.

I leaned down and saw the normal looking coin that Shelly was examining. Loose change wasn't anything special to me, we could go home and find that in the couch, but I pretended to be excited. "Wow, great. Can we go now?"

"Relax RJ, what're you so worried about?" she asked.

Shelly was staring at me, I could feel it. She waited for a response. But I didn't say anything and avoided eye contact with her. My head involuntarily turned back to look at the castle.

"Oh, come on. You're not *really* afraid of that place are you? There's nothing there. No one. What's so scary?"

No one had seen anyone living at the castle for years. But every time we got close to it, chills raced up my spine and I felt eyes watching my every move.

I tried to distract myself and think about anything else. My video games. The nice, happy books I liked to read. The lemonade stand that we had to go home and get ready for. That was it, I could think about that!

Our lemonade stand was another reason to turn back. Mom was probably waiting for us to go to the store to get the mix. It had been four years since we all built the first stand—when Dad was still here. Anyway, we had the system down. Each year our goal—well mine—was to make more money than the previous year. Shelly's was to gulp down the toxic yellow mix she called a magical potion.

I loved the lemonade stand—selling stuff to people was so fun. I felt like a grown up, instead of just a scared kid.

It was getting darker. Then, out of nowhere, crickets started to chirp, and an owl hooted!

My stomach clenched. I had to get out of here right away. "Come on!" I yelled to Shelly, but she was still examining her new coin.

"Alright, alright. I'm coming," she snapped.

Finally, I thought. *I would've left her here, but my mom would kill me if I came home without her.*

We turned and walked back to our house. Shelly stuck the coin into her pocket and patted the front of her jeans to make sure it was secure. As we walked, footsteps echoed our own. Or at least I thought they did. My throat started to dry up.

I looked behind us—nothing there. But it was very dark now. I couldn't shake the feeling of being followed. I picked up the pace. At least we were on our way home. Nothing else could go wrong.

While we walked, Shelly was quiet. Typically, she was talking my ear off about whatever new artifact she was bringing to the house. Eventually we were going to be able to have a museum of weird, scary stuff.

She was holding her hand firmly against her pocket, as if someone was about to run up and steal the coin from her jeans. "You really got a hold on that coin." I teased her. I laughed, even though it wasn't my best joke.

Expecting a response, I stared at her real close, but she never said anything. Not a thing, though her face looked a little red. Maybe sunburn, it was summer after all.

Shelly lost her footing, must've been a rock or something in her path, but that was also odd because normally I was the clumsy one. She tried to regain her balance but looked like she was walking along a tightrope in the circus — her arms were straight out as her body swayed.

Before I could reach out and steady her, Shelly collapsed to the ground.

At first, I thought that she had just tripped, and this was all nothing, but she didn't get back up. Instead, she wiggled around on the ground like jello would.

"The coin — my leg!" Shelly clawed at her thigh, like an animal caught in a trap. She panted as she spoke, unable to put together full sentences.

My mouth dropped open. I felt dizzy. "What's wrong?" I screamed frantically. "Are you okay? Shell?"

My mind jammed up like a shredder with too much paper in it—it was in overload. *What am I supposed to do?*

I bent down to help her up, but I couldn't pull her to her feet. Her legs weren't working. The coin! *Why did she pick up that stupid coin?*

I ripped her hand away from her pocket, freeing a path to the coin so that I could grab it and get it out of her jeans. That was all I could think of. If that didn't work, I was clueless.

My hand reached into her pocket. I pulled the coin out. My eyes scoured the area, looking for a place to trash it. I wanted it as far away from us as fast as possible.

A creepy, crackling whisper blew through the wind, *"The lake. Throw it in the lake."*

My body shuddered as I glanced toward the castle, trying to see beyond it to the water. Where was that voice coming from?

One more time, the voice tickled my ear hair. *"Throw it in the lake."*

The lake. Nothing would happen to us if I threw it into the lake.

But, it's the lake.

Would I even be able to get it there? *Stop thinking!* It was for Shelly. I had no choice.

No. I can't. No way.

8

"RJ ... *the lake,*" the whisper said my name!

I was spooked. I spun around, looking for anyone who could have said it, but there was nothing.

The coin started to turn bright green in my palm, appearing electrically charged, as if it was activating. I couldn't debate this any longer. I had to act.

I raced past the median toward the castle grounds and the gate. I reeled my arm back and released the coin, heaving my entire weight into the throw.

Creakkkkkkk.

The rusted fence nearly toppled as I crashed into it. I steadied myself so that I didn't fall onto the property while the coin raced through the sky like an airplane. But, before it had any chance of making it to the lake, it lost speed. Crash landing. The coin fell way short of the lake, landing instead in the tall, wild grass. It was still a good throw though, further than I thought it would have gone.

And, at least the coin was out of our hands.

I rushed back to Shelly, who lay stiff on the ground. "Nooooooo!" Sweat fell from my forehead. My hands shook as I reached out to check her pulse. *Be okay. Please. Don't die on me.*

I wasn't sure how to help her. How could a coin do this?

Suddenly, Shelly's eyes opened, and she jumped up. "Gotcha!" she dusted herself off like nothing had happened.

My heart had to be beating 10,000 times a second. My hat flew off my head—the only thing saving it from being lost forever was the hat's black string wrapped around my neck. I nearly fainted. I hated my sister when she did these things to me. Being scared was the worst.

It felt like my skin was on fire. I was so mad that I didn't say a word. I wanted to yell and scream, but Shelly was never going to change.

"Oh, come on, be a good sport," she egged me on while we continued walking home. "You cost me a nice piece for my collection. And you couldn't even make it into the lake."

"Yes, I could," I yelled. "But I was worried about you. I just didn't get a good enough running start."

"Like that would have mattered! I bet I could throw as far as the lake," she teased, then reached down and grabbed a rock from the dirt. "Watch." Shelly ran toward the castle grounds.

"No! Let's go home!" I screamed, but this didn't stop Shelly from sprinting away.

I watched helplessly as she ran to the gate. She didn't look like she was going to stop. Oh no, this was going to be the day that she stepped inside the gates. "No, Shell!" I yelled, hoping that she wasn't actually going to do it. She didn't stop. Her small, skinny frame slid underneath one of the loose parts of the fence and she ran through the weeds, past where I threw the coin.

What was she thinking? She was much closer to the lake than I had been, but still too far away for throwing the rock into the lake. She pulled her arm back, ready to throw, but suddenly bright lights flooded the area. Shelly stopped abruptly and turned. Her face went pale. Her hand opened and the rock fell to the ground.

Aughhhhhh! We were caught! I didn't want to find out by whom. "Run!" I yelled.

She dashed toward me but slowed down as she passed the spot where the coin had landed. I wasn't waiting. I was gone, running as fast as I could. She caught up to me really fast, like she had supersonic speed. We were moving so fast, we might've broken an Olympic record. It felt like the lights were tracking us, but how?

I couldn't look back. Fear had cemented my neck facing forward. That was why I never wanted to go onto that property. Someone or something could be there. Who knew? What if whatever was there saw us? What if it was waiting for us to come back?

My natural survival instincts kicked in and helped keep me from thinking about how exhausting this run was. Our path was illuminated by the lights that came from directly behind us. We had to get somewhere safe fast. My lungs were burning as my legs slowed down. I couldn't run much farther. If something was chasing me, I was as good as caught.

Shelly slowed down and looked back toward the castle. A big smile spread across her face and she laughed.

"Are you crazy?" I yelled, gasping for air as I passed by her in a slow jog. "What's wrong with you?"

"Look." She pointed, while laughter escaped her tiny mouth. But, I couldn't. I couldn't turn back.

A black SUV with tinted windows drove by with its headlights cutting through the night.

"It was a car." Shelly bent over her belly laugh. "You were so scared! What did you think was going to happen? Some ghost was gonna come out and grab us?"

Shelly's piercing laugh taunted me like the buzzing mosquitos trying to eat my flesh. I swatted at them, much like I dismissed Shelly's cackle. I'd had enough. Walks with Shelly were too emotional sometimes.

The vehicle slowly drove past. Were they looking at us? Through the dark windows? Whoever was driving hit the gas pedal and sped off, exiting the neighborhood. I finally stopped and glanced back. The castle was out of view and dark. The lights had definitely come from the SUV, but where was it coming from? The castle?

I walked faster, wiping the sweat from my forehead as I made it to the light of our front door. That's where I waited for Shelly. If anything else happened it would be easy to run inside.

She was across the lawn, still grabbing her stomach, laughing so hard. It was like a pull-string doll's laugh—loud and obnoxious. Finally, she crossed the grass, stepped onto the doormat, and walked inside the house. I looked one last time toward the castle.

The neighborhood was completely dark, but I could see something. Red dots in the distance that appeared to be moving closer to the house. What were they?

Wait a second … were those eyes?

CHAPTER TWO

I rushed inside, slammed the door, and held it shut with my back to make sure it would stay closed even if a hurricane blew through the neighborhood.

What the heck was out there? Those red dots were eyes ... I think. But where was the body of whoever had stalked us? My heart raced. I tightly crossed my arms across my chest to help slow my rapid breathing.

I couldn't think about it anymore. I'd drive myself crazy. We were safe at home now, nothing to worry about here. But first, I deadbolted the door and made sure the blue curtain was covering the window in the door. Extra security never hurt anyone.

I took a deep breath. Shelly and Mom were talking in the kitchen. They sure sounded excited.

One last time, I shifted the blue curtain to the side and looked outside. Nothing. I shook my head and wandered into the next room. Mom had already started preparing for our annual lemonade stand and had a batch made for us to try.

"The best!" Shelly threw her arms into the air after tasting it. The sweeter the lemonade, the more enthusiastic her reaction was. Shelly was always about the product. But me, I loved the planning and preparation. I was thinking of which snacks we should sell, cup sizes, and how much we should charge to maximize our cash.

When we finished the first stand, our parents let us keep the money. We were allowed to buy whatever we wanted. I think I bought a few kazoos and some candy bars, maybe a board game. My sister ended up with some sort of stuffed monster or doll. Then Mom encouraged us to consider others instead of buying things for ourselves like the cell phones we always asked for. So since the first stand, we donated the money to different causes.

One year we let Shelly choose the charity, and we ended up giving the money to a local farm for Halloween hayrides. Because we donated, they gave us a free ride. Luckily for me, the hayrides weren't the haunted kind.

This year we chose a group that gave toys to children in need during the holidays. Who wanted to be a kid that couldn't have toys? That seemed wrong to me.

I tried a taste of the lemonade, too. It was fine. I never loved lemonade, but I loved the stand. It was time to go anyway, we had to get more supplies before it got too late. One last sip by my sister and we were off to the store.

Mom, Shelly, and I strolled through the aisles of our local grocery store. We had to get more of the mix, and cookies and snacks that we thought would keep people at our stand. The saltier the snack, the more lemonade they needed to drink to quench their thirst.

Maybe I actually was a businessman in the making. I wanted to raise more money than we'd ever had before. Records were about to be shattered. Our highest total so far was $64.50. We'd need to sell quite a bit of lemonade to beat it, but I had faith.

When Shelly and my mom stopped at the deli counter, I left them to look around. I scanned the aisles: fresh fruit, pasta, sauces, soups, paper products. Then I reached the snacks. There was everything from pretzels to popcorn. What were the best ones to keep our customers drinking lemonade?

I grabbed a bag of tortilla chips and the saltiest pretzels I could find. As I headed for the registers to meet Mom and Shelly, a chill swept over me, even though I was nowhere near the freezer section.

I stopped and looked around. People were going about their shopping like nothing was happening. They didn't appear to be cold, but hypothermia attacked my body. The chill spread through my insides. I backed up a few steps, hoping that it would disappear. Coldness enveloped my every move, no matter which direction I went in.

I was in shorts and a t-shirt because it was almost eighty degrees outside, but I was shaking, and goosebumps rose on my body. Instinctively, I dropped the bags of snacks, and pulled the brim of my hat over my eyes. Then I hugged myself tightly to try to warm up. Why was I so cold?

A scratching noise destroyed my eardrums—the sound that someone makes when they claw their fingernails along a chalkboard. *Shrieeeeeeeeeek.*

Augh. I broke my bear hug to cover my ears. My body cringed as the sound started, then stopped, then started, then stopped. Where was the sound coming from? Did anyone else hear this? No one was reacting like they had heard it.

Right then my worst nightmare showed up at the wrong time. Johnny from school walked by the aisle I was standing in. He saw me.

My eyes met his as Johnny pointed and laughed hysterically at me. "Aww, everything okay?" He teased. Why did he always pick on me? It felt like school during the summer time. This was supposed to be my break from him. What was he going to do, put me in the cooler with the milk and eggs?

But for once, I was fortunate. He was with his family, otherwise I'm sure he would have tormented me more. His dad knocked him lightly in the head to stop his comments and they kept walking out of sight.

Shrieeeeekkkkk!

Augh! There it was again! I wasn't really sure what to do, but Mom and Ed always encouraged me to be braver. So against my own will, I lifted the brim of my hat above my eyes and walked toward the noise. I reached the end cap of the aisle, which was filled with bags of potato chips.

I really had no idea what I was about to see. I hoped that someone's faulty grocery cart was out of control crashing into things in the aisle. Yes, that was what it was going to be. What was I so worried about? *We're at the grocery store with people around, none of them are nervous.* Then I saw what was causing the sound. I stopped dead.

There it was. A cane unlike any I'd ever seen before. It was black with weird designs engraved into the shaft. It was tall with a roundish top that looked like a skull to hold on to. The bottom tapered to a point sharp enough to shred my bones like paper.

I pushed my head deeper into the display of potato chips, pressing my face against the plastic packaging. From this angle, I could still see around the corner without actually getting closer. Black boots with metal straps came into view. With each step, the boots jingled like Santa Claus' bag at Christmas. But this didn't feel like my favorite holiday—it felt more like Halloween.

Slowly, my eyes wandered upward. Black pants. A long, hanging trench coat. A bright red glove grasping the top of the cane. My heart raced. My body trembled and I opened my eyes as wide as I possibly could.

I didn't want to look up any further. I didn't want whoever this was to be staring back at me, waiting for me to come around the corner. I'd been brave enough for one day—I'd peeked at something scary, but that was it for me.

I couldn't do it. I couldn't look anymore.

I hid my eyes under the brim of my hat again and tucked my head back into the chips. Deep breath after deep breath escaped from my mouth, like I was hyperventilating. I tried to compose myself. Sweat dripped. Chills continued. I hated how scared I was all the time. I needed to get myself calm before my mom or Shelly saw me. Maybe I should've run. What if this person was coming my way?

I tried to get myself back to normal by thinking happy thoughts—the lemonade stand again, my mom, Shelly, my books, my video games.

Breathe, RJ.

I couldn't focus. Everything around me was spinning. I felt like I was outside my body. *This can't be real. Everything's going to be fine.*

Something grabbed me.

I closed my eyes and screamed at the top of my lungs.

CHAPTER THREE

I'm having a heart attack! Twelve-years-old, and I was going to die in the middle of the grocery store. My obituary would read: RJ the scaredy-cat died between the frozen foods and the snacks. I had hoped I'd make it through at least another twelve years, but it wasn't looking good.

The hand grabbing me felt familiar.

There was no glove touching me. The fingers felt like the ones that had scratched my back as a kid while I fell asleep. The palm was the same one that held my hand when I was younger and crossing the street. The motion of the hand was the same as the one that had rubbed my shoulders to comfort me when Dad died.

Slowly, I turned and got only a glimpse of the shopping cart because my hat had shielded my view. Gradually, I lifted the brim higher. It was my mom.

"RJ, why are you yelling?" Mom looked around, hoping that I wasn't causing a scene. "Come on, we gotta go. Ed's waiting for us at home." Mom stared at me, probably wondering what was wrong with me.

Great, Ed's there now. Mom's probably going to make this even worse for me. She'll probably tell him all about the grocery store. He'll probably want me to talk to him for hours about what *exactly* scared me. So annoying.

"Are you really scared at the grocery store?" Mom asked. "I thought we were working on this. You're almost a teenager. You have to try and be less scared, honey. Besides, you're in a *grocery store*. What are you worried about?" She sounded a little frustrated as she rested her arm around my shoulder. "Maybe it's time for another talk with Ed. Really open up to him. You know he works with children."

There wasn't anything I could say, so I nodded, hoping she wouldn't make me talk to Ed. I knew it was weird, but she hadn't seen what I had. Besides, at this point, she'd think I was overreacting like every other time I was scared. After a few glances over my shoulder to make sure we weren't being followed, I felt safe again, hoping that I never saw whatever I'd seen, again.

Later that night, Shelly and I put the finishing touches on our lemonade special. It was a blindingly bright, toxic yellow. I imagined how delicious it was. I couldn't wait to try it, and neither could Shelly. She was still mixing with her long plastic spoon, as if she were kayaking through the jar of lemonade. It was ready, but before we tasted it, we always let Mom try first. It was our tradition.

Mom came into the kitchen wearing one of her purple scrub shirts from work. During her work days, she helped people, but on the eve of the lemonade stand, she was always the first victim—I mean, customer.

I filled a small cup and handed it to my mother. She smelled the potent lemonade and took a swig. Her face turned bright red as she swirled the lemonade in her mouth. She held it in her mouth like a squirrel hoarding food for winter. Her eyebrows raised and her lips pressed together as she let out a loud whistling noise.

We needed to add more water.

Shelly and Mom filled up the pitchers as Ed walked into the kitchen. He slowly strutted in. His crooked smile caught my attention. "I heard we may have to have a little talk, young man. Heard something got you spooked at the grocery store."

I bowed my head. The moment I dreaded was here. "I'm fine," I blurted out, hoping he'd know that was my "leave me alone" tone. What was I going to tell him? Some monster or something was in the aisle next to me with a cane that was probably going to go through my body? I'm not trying to sound crazy here.

He came closer and reached out his arm, then put it over my shoulder. I tensed up trying to knock it off. *Ugh, why is he touching me?*

Beep! Beep! Beep! Ed's cell phone went off. He quickly checked his phone. "It's the hospital. I gotta go. We'll continue this later." He looked sternly at me and then, was gone.

With Mom's help, we compromised on the taste and then went to bed, though I bet she added more water to the pitchers while we were asleep. We had so much lemonade and way too many customers the next day.

Or maybe I should say: one too many.

*   *   *

I shot out of bed the next morning. I was so excited that I'd slept in my baggy cargo shorts. I wore those so I could fit all of the money in my pockets. We also had a jar for coins, but I was always prepared in case we ran out of places to keep the money. Lemonade stand day was my favorite—used to be, anyway.

I grabbed my hat and put it on my head, then rushed out of my room and knocked on my sister's door. Shelly was ready, too. She grabbed her purple fanny pack with a skull on it, tied her hair up in with a yellow band, and ran down the stairs in her mismatched outfit.

As I opened the front door, sunlight instantly warmed my body, and the air smelled crisp and clean. It was beautiful out. A perfect day for a lemonade stand!

We each had two large pitchers of lemonade when Mom stumbled down the stairs, rubbing the tiredness from her eyes. She brought out the folding table for us. She was also there to talk to the neighbors because we didn't have time for that. Besides, what would we talk to them about? Something cool? Yeah, right.

Mom quickly set up the table at the end of our driveway. Then my sister and I placed the pitchers on top and hung our beautiful sign: *Lemonade 50¢.*

We used the same sign every year. The words had started to fade over the years, and the red paint that we used to write 'lemonade' and the price had started to run. It looked a little like blood. Not the message I was trying to get across, but Shelly was okay with that.

"The best!" Shelly yelled as she slammed back one of the small cups and chucked it into our garbage can.

Our next-door neighbors, the Swansons, were among the first to arrive. They were often the ones entrusted with keeping an eye on us when Mom was gone. That was supposed to be the case for later that night, as Mom and Ed were going to an event, but Shelly and I convinced them to leave us home alone. The Swansons were the nicest couple, but had such a sad story. Their twelve-year-old son Wally went missing a few years after they came to town. That was long before we ever moved in. Wally was never found, although the Swansons searched everywhere for him. It was still a mystery.

I often wondered why they didn't have more kids of their own. I never asked them about it, because I'm sure it makes them sad to think about Wally, but I probably would've been friends with their kid.

All of our other neighbors came by, said hi, and bought cups of lemonade.

Even Ed showed up at the stand. I wasn't sure if he was going to come out and support us, but he did. He wandered over to us and put some money in the jar, but he didn't drink any lemonade.

"Are you doing okay today?" Ed asked, while standing in front of me at the table.

"Yeah, of course. I'm fine," I responded, hoping someone would come up and need more lemonade so I could get out of this awkward situation.

Ed barely showed any emotion when he responded. "We should still talk. I think your mom would like that."

"Whatever," I said, pacing around, looking behind him as a new group of people approached. "We have customers."

Ugh. What the heck. Leave me alone, especially today. Every day he was on me, but he couldn't give me a break on lemonade stand day? I wanted to yell, "You're not my dad," but what good would that do?

The day went on and the stand was winding down. We had a jar full of money to donate to the charity, and we were running low on lemonade, partially because Shelly couldn't stop chugging it down. Jeez, it was as if she'd eaten a bag of pretzels before we set everything up. I kept giving her a look, but she didn't care. She might as well have stuck her tongue out at me each time she drank another full cup.

Out of nowhere, a breeze blew and the sky changed from blue to purple in a matter of seconds. Then it was dark and grey, and the whole day changed. The perfect eighty-degree summer day was shifting. A storm was approaching.

I looked at all of the people gathered around the stand. They kept talking and didn't seem to notice. Neither did Mom, but it looked like Shelly looked at me, up at the sky, and then smirked. She seemed excited. She loved thunderstorms.

Ed was talking with the Swansons. He stood tall next to them with a crooked, scheming smile on his face. Weird, because Ed never talked to anyone else in the neighborhood. I wasn't even sure the Swansons knew who he was, but maybe he was just introducing himself. For whatever reason, butterflies filled my stomach.

To make matters worse, Johnny, Brad, and Coleman from school were riding their bikes up to the stand. What were they doing here? They always hassled me at school, I hoped that they wouldn't do that to me at home too. The three of them pointed directly at me. I could feel tension fill the air. "RJ, let's go!" Johnny yelled. "We're going to number 13."

"Yeah, come on, or you too scared?" Brad chimed in.

They laughed and cheered amongst themselves. They weren't funny. Why did they think they were? No one at the stand seemed to notice, except Shelly. She ran out into the street after them and yelled, "Yeah, go see house 13. See what happens!"

They didn't look back. They kept pedaling toward the old scary castle and I smiled. It was definitely going to rain and they were going to get trapped in it. Finally, a win for me against the bullies.

Darkness covered the sun. Thunder roared and lightning struck—I think. Of course, I hated that part. The wind whipped, nearly blowing over the whole table. I grabbed it and held on so it wouldn't topple over. Why wasn't anyone else afraid of this storm?

I struggled to see through the darkness. Did the bullies make it to the castle? Then two beady, dark red beams stared back at me, headed in my direction.

My knees buckled. If it weren't for holding onto the table, my body would've collapsed like a ton of bricks. Chills shook me on this warm, summer afternoon. I might as well have looked straight into Medusa's eyes. It would have been better if I had turned into stone right then and there. Instead, as the red beams got closer, I realized that something was headed toward me.

Quickly, I broke eye contact just as my mom saw my face. Didn't she see it, too? She put her hand on my shoulder. "What's wrong?"

I couldn't talk. My eyes darted back towards the creature headed my way, trying to motion for my mother. *Look!* I thought. *Can't you see? I'm not crazy, am I?*

She never looked, then one of the neighbors called her over. Mom left and started talking with them.

Mom … noooo!

Was this the same thing that I saw at the grocery store?

The creature approached. It was a man. He was so tall, much taller than Ed, but he was mangy and dirty like a coyote, but moved like a squid lost on land. His eyes were dark, blood red and sunken deep into a plastic grey mask. Then I saw the sharp end of the cane from the store. It was him. He was back for me.

He got closer. His blistered lips bubbled like the top of a hot pepperoni pizza, oozing grease everywhere. Fresh sores formed as I stared.

What was he doing here?

How did no one else see this?

I pulled my gaze away as fast as I could, hoping that he didn't see me.

But he did.

Slowly, he squirmed towards the stand. As he approached, people robotically parted but without seeing him, and he walked through the middle of the crowd.

I wanted to scream. This was like being on the scariest rollercoaster ever, about to go down a steep drop. Maybe I could push the table over. If I knocked it over, then there wouldn't be any lemonade for him. Why did he want our lemonade anyway? He didn't. There was no way that he was here for that.

Five yards away.

I got a whiff of his aroma. It reminded me of my grandparent's old, scary cellar: mold, mildew, dry rot, fungus.

Four yards …

His creepy stare was fixed on me. His eyes were like laser beams locked on a target. I couldn't break away. I begged my legs to move, but they were mysteriously glued to the ground. I wanted to scream at my feet: *Run, he's coming.*

Three yards …

His cane scraped against the blacktop, leaving small scratches as he got closer and closer to the table.

Two yards …

My sister noticed my fright, looked at me, then at him.

I'm not crazy. She saw him too.

Didn't she?

One yard …

AUGH!

CHAPTER FOUR

This creature, whatever it was, stared at me. Through me. His hand disappeared into his pocket. I couldn't imagine that he was reaching for anything good. I doubted that he would pull out a new video game, shake my hand, and ask to be friends.

What was he doing here? Was he here for me? Maybe my sister. Was this because Shelly had been on thirteen's property earlier? Was he watching us?

Red gloves poked through the ends of his dark jacket sleeves. His bony fingers protruded through holes in the gloves. Gloves that he was wearing during the summer. Did he not feel the heat? There was no need for a jacket or gloves, unless he was hiding something ...

As he dug deep into his left pocket, change clanked. He pulled his hand out and emptied the coins into the jar. He'd added extra, but I was too afraid to tell him. I trusted that he gave enough and quickly poured a cup of lemonade. Heck, I would've given him the whole batch if he wanted it, especially if that would have gotten him to leave.

I put the lemonade on the table in front of him. I couldn't look away. Slowly and methodically, like a robot, he picked up the cup and raised it to his covered face. His scaly lips were exposed by the mask, and he had just enough room to drink from the cup. Lemonade dribbled from the corner of his mouth and dripped down his covered face. He reached up with his right hand and wiped it, smearing a reddish substance on his mask. He looked like a toddler trying to finger paint with blood.

Oh no, did he just finish impaling someone with his cane? Was I next?

The world around me didn't seem real. It was a haze, like some ghostly mirage. Did my sister or anyone else see this? I couldn't look to find out. I was too worried that something would happen to me if I took my eyes off of him.

The creature never changed his expression. He never spoke. Then he turned and disappeared into the distance, scraping his cane across the pavement. I was left hoping that this was the last time I'd see him.

*   *   *

As everything with the stand finished up, I tried to refocus on our goal. It had been a successful day, yet I had no idea if we'd broken our record. But thoughts of the creature, The Impaler, as I called him, still plagued my mind.

While cleaning up, I grabbed Shelly's arm and whispered, "You saw him today right? The creepy guy?" Or did I see a ghost?

"What are you talking about?" Shelly responded. I rolled my eyes. I wasn't trying to make a big deal out of this. I didn't want Mom and Ed to think I was still a scaredy-cat. But Shelly kept going on and on. "RJ—you're twelve. There are no ghosts." She shook her head and rushed over to the lemonade pitchers to drink the leftovers.

Shelly was in some mood, but how had she not seen him? I hoped that she was just distracted because at the end of the day, she was allowed to drink the last of the lemonade. As if she hadn't had enough already.

I knew I saw The Impaler. But why didn't anyone else? Why was I different?

Shelly and I collected all of our leftover supplies, while Mom and Ed brought the table

34

inside. We put everything away and grabbed the coins to count, but they wanted to talk with us before they left for their event.

"Now I know you've been home by yourselves a couple times," Mom began, "but it's been during the day. Are you sure you're going to be okay if we leave you for a few hours at night? We'll be back later, but you both should be in bed. Otherwise, you could stay at the Swansons' house. They'd be glad to have you at their place instead, if you're scared."

Both my sister and I assured them that we'd be fine. "You know I won't be afraid," Shelly added.

"RJ, are you gonna be okay in charge? Are you ready to be brave?" Ed asked, while Mom nudged him.

"Yes, we'll be fine." I was annoyed that he always reminded me of how scared I usually was.

"I thought that's why we sent RJ to school to learn about CPR," Shelly chimed in. "Besides, I'm here. So there's nothing to worry about."

I rolled my eyes at her comment. But I didn't care that much, whatever got Ed out of the house was okay with me, even if it meant that Mom went, too. I was looking forward to a night without chores and with lots of video games. None of that would scare me.

Mom finally agreed to let us stay home alone. Apparently Ed was getting some award for his research. He never told us exactly what kind of studies he did, but Mom said he worked with kids. I wondered why Ed never included us in any of his work, not that I wanted to spend more time than I had to with him.

Mom talked to us one last time about behaving and kissed us what felt like a gazillion times. "Now RJ, you know that you're allowed to call us if something happens, but please make sure it's an emergency. This is an important event that Ed and I are going to, so make sure you really need us." Mom grabbed her purse from the counter.

"We'll be fine, don't worry," I assured them, knowing I had to act tough. Besides, I was already planning which video game to play first.

After what felt like an eternity, they walked out the door and locked it. Finally, we were free and able to do whatever we wanted for the next few hours. What first?

I looked out the window again to make sure that they were gone. Brad and Coleman were pedaling with a sense of urgency as they rushed out of the neighborhood. Where was Johnny? Hopefully he wasn't headed here to mess with me. He was always the worst of the three. I wished one day that I could get revenge.

I kept staring, making sure that if Johnny was going to stop by, I would be ready. But he wasn't anywhere to be found and it was getting late. I squinted my eyes to adjust to the blackened sky. I reached over and hit the switch for the outside lights.

Augh! Dark red dots came into view, moving closer to our house. I looked harder, deeper—it was *him*. He was back.

CHAPTER FIVE

Tingles ran across my body. Goosebumps raced to the surface of my skin. I stammered my words trying to talk to Shelly as she told me what she wanted to do while Mom was gone. I couldn't focus. Her voice was muffled in the background. I was fixated on him.

What was he doing here? Watching us? Did he know that we were by ourselves?

Questions filled my head, but I didn't want to say them out loud. I was too scared. It was difficult trying to be fearless—to not worry about everything. I didn't need Shelly, my younger sister, to help me be brave ... did I?

He stood outside as I looked out at him through the window. He cocked his head and stared directly at me again. Each time his eyes met mine, it felt like he was stripping my mind of its contents. Like he was going through my brain the way kids unloaded their toy chests—all at once, until they found what they were looking for.

I shut the blinds and ran through the kitchen, up the stairs, and to my room. I closed the door and dove into my bed, then tucked myself under the covers and shielded my eyes with the brim of my hat. I wasn't sure of what to do. Shelly was already off doing her own thing. But, my head wasn't completely under the covers. I was, at least, being a little brave. My ears perked up, listening intently for any unusual noises.

Seconds passed. Then minutes. I coached myself to get up and watch some TV so I could try to enjoy my night without leaving the safety of my bedroom. I lifted the brim of my hat so that I could see my television.

Ding dong. The doorbell! My body seized and my eyebrows rose in fear.

"I'll get it," Shelly yelled and ran from her room like she was competing in an Olympic event.

"Wait," I yelled after her as I ripped open my door. But I was too late, she was already down the stairs.

Oh no, I thought, *what could he want? Why would he be coming to our house?*

Shelly turned the handle and opened the door, while I walked down the stairs and cowered behind her. Cautiously, I peered around her to see who was standing there.

Shelly smiled, which reassured me that it was okay. The Swansons were standing at the front door. Phew!

But where was The Impaler? Hesitantly, I peeked my head out of the door and looked left then right to see if he was around. But he was gone. What the heck? Was I imagining all of this stuff?

"Do you guys want to come over for dinner?" Melinda Swanson asked.

"Ahhh," Shelly looked up to me. I shrugged my shoulders, but she responded, "No, I think we're good! Thanks though!"

"You sure?" Mrs. Swanson tried again.

"Yeah! We'll be okay!" I called out.

"Alright! Well if you need anything, we're right next door!"

Shelly and I waved goodbye then closed the door.

"Let's count the cash!" Shelly called out.

Somehow, I had almost forgotten about the cash. Shelly was right, it was time to count our money, quarter by quarter, dollar by dollar.

We dumped all of our earnings on the table. I hunched over from my chair, close to the change, so focused on counting that it was hurting my neck. I moved my head back and forth, trying to stretch it out and ease the pain. I wiped my eyes and looked at Shelly while she counted. She was pale, sickly looking. Her hands shook as she grabbed for more coins.

"What's wrong with you?"

"What are you talking about? I'm counting," Shelly snapped, not looking up.

"Why do you look like that?" I reached out to touch her forehead, feeling for a fever.

She pulled away and shot up from the table. "What are you doing? This is how I look." Shelly yelled then stared me down. I couldn't help but notice her eyes. They were darkening. Reddening. So were her arms. It seemed like whatever it was, was spreading.

Shelly had never looked like this before. I was caught off guard and raised my voice to match the volume of hers. "No, you don't. Go upstairs and look in the mirror. I'll wait for you to keep counting."

She groaned, stormed off, and stomped up the stairs—slamming her feet into each step individually. She disappeared for a few minutes. I waited for her, hoping that everything was okay. I really didn't want to deal with anything else today. Then she came rushing back down the stairs.

The color had returned to her face, and she looked normal again. "You look much better," I said. "What was wrong?"

She shrugged. "Nothing RJ, you worry too much."

Shelly seemed slightly happier. *I don't know,* I thought. *Maybe I was imagining things again. A minute ago she was mean and looked ready to throw up. But then she was fine. Was my mind playing tricks on me?*

We counted the last coin then added up the piles. It was a tie. Exactly the same as last year. How was that possible?

Then Shelly said, "Wait a second, I almost forgot." She pulled out two quarters from her pocket and put them on the table. "$65," she said. "The best!" She reached out and high-fived me. I smacked her hand back. We did it!

I went into the living room and played one of my newest adventure video games. Those were the best kind of games. They made me feel like I could do anything—exactly how the characters I was controlling could. They were never scared and it was fun to imagine myself like that. Brave.

I got lost in those games. My attention was nearly unbreakable. I saw nothing else. Heard nothing else. Until, that is, a blood curdling scream ripped through the house.

My own adventure was about to begin, whether I wanted it to or not.

CHAPTER SIX

I jumped up from the carpeted floor. The controller fell from my hands and smashed against the ground, sending the batteries flying across the room. I looked to the stairs and hesitantly called out, "Shelly?"

Why did this happen on my watch? This wasn't fair. I had to go up there. This better not be a prank.

I felt my throat tighten as Shelly screamed again. I tried to swallow, but the walls of my throat refused to accept my own spit.

Slowly, I walked to the closet near the stairs. Finally, after all these years of keeping my stuff in here, it would pay off. *What should I grab? The hammer?*

I opened the closet door. *Jackets? A suitcase? A lab coat?*

Are you kidding me? Where was my stuff? Ed had replaced my stuff with his!

Another scream destroyed my eardrums. *Oh no.*

This was it. I had to run.

My legs burned as my feet trampled up the stairs. I rushed into Shelly's room. Her face was so red I could barely tell the difference between her and a tomato. Tears rushed down her face, each one racing to see which could get to her chin faster.

"What's wrong?" My voice squealed with fear.

Shelly was sitting in bed, hunched over, with her black covers tossed to the side. She couldn't talk yet. She was panting from crying and screaming. Her chest rose and fell rapidly. I didn't know what to do. She was a wreck. I grabbed her and hugged her.

Finally, she got control of herself and was able to talk. "My face, what's wrong with my face?" Shelly asked frantically, pushing me away, and pointing to her cheek.

"What are you talking about?" There wasn't anything different with her face except for the color, but that was returning to its normal, pinkish hue. To me, she looked okay.

"RJ, don't joke!"

"I'm not, I swear. Look in the mirror," I pointed to the bathroom.

Shelly got up and hurried to examine herself in the mirror. She pointed her cheek closer towards her reflection as if afraid she'd missed whatever she thought was going on.

I tried not to look around her room too much while she was gone, but I couldn't help it. She had so many weird things scattered around: her shrunken head from our beach vacation, a new pet spider, and the human skull decoration that she got from the mall. How could she live like this? No wonder she was freaking out. One of these things probably came to life and attacked her. *Flying fishsticks*, this place gave me the heebie jeebies.

She walked back into her room and sat on the bed next to me. "Wow, that was some nightmare."

I sighed and rubbed my hand on top of my hat, adjusting it to sit normally on my head. "Yeah, you scared the crud out of me."

"Nothing new there." Shelly would forever tease me.

"Ha-ha … guess you're feeling better."

Shelly looked at my hat, which was still a little crooked. She reached up and fixed it so that it was straight. "You look like him from some of the pictures I've seen."

"Thanks." She was talking about Dad. "Do you remember him?" I asked.

"A little bit, but mostly from the stories that you and Mom told me. Otherwise, I only remember a few things, like that time we went fishing by our old house," Shelly said, sitting up with a smile. "Remember those little canoes and our small fishing poles?"

"Yeah." I could remember it like it was yesterday. We were out on the water all day and the only person who caught anything was Dad, and it was only one fish—a small guppy that we threw back.

"And you always make me think of him when you say flying fishsticks." Shelly let loose a big smile.

"Dad always said that when he was mad or frustrated, probably his way of cursing around us," I said.

"Well it gets more use now, since you say it when you're scared."

I shrugged, wanting to tease her back, but I wasn't great at that. I just thought about Dad. He was a professional fisherman. We moved here because there were a few opportunities with the lake nearby—the one behind thirteen's house. Dad loved it. He took me once on a small motorboat, just the two of us. We went far out on the lake and caught tons of fish. It was a blast. I probably would have gone a bunch more times with him too, but he never made it back from his last trip.

The boat sank and Dad disappeared into the lake. No one ever found his body, just his yellow bucket hat, which was why I wore it. The hat was all I had left of my dad. My father's death was the reason why I hated that lake and being anywhere near it. The lake was dangerous. It seemed like anything that ever got lost in there was gone forever. That was the reason why I never liked going near thirteen's house. It was way too close to the lake.

Shelly nudged me, "You okay?"

My thoughts cleared. I looked at her and half-smiled, "Yeah, just thinking about him. You okay?"

"Yeah, I think I'm fine." She lay back down and sighed.

I patted her on the shoulder, reassuringly. Then I went to use the bathroom. I took a minute and looked into the mirror. I pointed my cheek closer to my reflection in case there was anything weird on me. Nothing.

What a day, I thought while splashing water onto my face. I dried off with a towel and left the bathroom. I wandered back into her room, which was now dimly lit from the small nightlight on the desk by her bed. Shelly was already asleep.

I went to my room and collapsed onto my bed. At this point, video games were not an option anymore. I didn't want to be awake. I hoped to get some sleep—to wake up back before we ever moved to this neighborhood, to have Mom and Dad home, and for everything to be okay. But that wasn't going to happen. I tossed and turned, wondering if I'd ever get comfortable. *Will I ever be able to sleep again?*

Hoping to calm my mind, I sat up and read. Yet the words on the page jumbled together. My brain couldn't make sense of what was right in front of me. All I could think about was my sister's scream. It haunted me. She never screamed like that. What if there was something actually wrong with her?

I couldn't sleep. My heart was racing. Furiously, I forced myself out of bed, turned on the lights, and took a few deep breaths. I needed to walk around because I was going crazy inside.

And Shelly—I had to check on her again to make sure she was okay. I'd be dead if anything happened to her while Mom was gone. But more importantly, I kind of liked my sister, so I didn't want anything to happen to her.

Carpet filled the spaces between my toes as I slowly walked down the hallway, tiptoeing to my sister's room. Everything was going to be fine, I reassured myself.

CHAPTER SEVEN

I tiptoed into her room slowly. Her body was slightly lit from the small nightlight and the outline of her face barely showed in the darkness.

I had to get a closer look. I leaned my head in and gasped.

Her face was masked with lesion upon lesion. One after another. There were volcanic eruptions taking place on Shelly's face.

"NOOOOOOOOO!" I yelled.

I grabbed Shelly by the shoulders and pulled her up from the pillow. Something flew out of her hand and slammed into the wall. Her eyes flew open. She looked scared beyond belief, like she could have died right then and there, and it was my doing, but it wasn't intentional. I was more terrified than I'd ever been in my life.

Otherwise, it would have been a proud moment when I'd finally scared my sister.

I sat her up and watched as the lesions on her face started to heal. What was happening to her? What was going on? How could these things be disappearing before my eyes? I pounded the bed with my fist. I was so mad, so confused, so frustrated.

"What the heck is wrong with you? Are you trying to kill me?" Shelly started to freak out and threw a pillow in my face. Then she looked at the sores covering her arms and legs.

We both stood up. I rubbed my eyes and she rubbed her face. There was nothing on Shelly's face anymore, but they were everywhere else. For the first time, Shelly looked lost, like she didn't know what to do.

I noticed something glowing by the far wall. It was electric green around the edges and the shape of a circle, but it seemed to be losing charge. "What is that?" I asked, pointing to the object.

"Nothing, it's mine!" Shelly dove after it. Thunder roared and lightning struck outside the moment that she touched the object. A loud crash shook the neighborhood. My heart leapt in my throat as my teeth rattled from the thunderous boom. The room went black.

"The power!" Shelly cried.

I flicked every light switch and lamp on. Nothing worked. My eyes shot around the darkness. I looked down the hallway then outside. The whole neighborhood was black.

The power was out.

Shelly's hands glowed in the darkness and the same blisters that were on her arms, shot up on her face again.

"What are you doing? Drop that!" I yelled, freaking out on her this time. She shot upright, scared of the sight of the blisters and my tone. I had never spoken to her like that.

I felt the ground. It was as hot as an oven, but I knelt down on it, ignoring the heat. I got closer and saw that the object was a coin of some sort. It was changing in front of my eyes. The green edges slowly disappeared.

I reached into her desk drawer and pulled out a flashlight. I clicked it on and shed light onto the coin on the bed.

It was a shiny, normal coin. I had no idea where the green edges were or what caused it to glow. I was perplexed. Why did it change? "This isn't the coin from the other day, is it? The one from thirteen?"

Shelly remained quiet. I had my answer.

"I thought I threw it into the yard. How did you get it?"

"I grabbed it before we ran away from the lights. It was lying in the grass."

"After all that, you still needed to bring it here?" I stared at Shelly.

"I needed it. It called to me. I thought it'd be perfect for my collection."

"Look at your arms," I said, pointing at them, "does that seem worth it?"

"It was never like this. My arms got red, but I thought they were just itchy or something."

"Do they hurt?"

Shelly shook her head.

I inched my hand toward her arms. Then I touched them. I hoped whatever this was, wasn't contagious. "Does that hurt?"

"A little."

I let out a sigh, wondering what was going on. "Why isn't the coin green anymore?"

"It's only green when you touch it. Watch." Shelly reached out and grabbed it. She winced in pain. It burned her hand, but she held it in her palm. The coin was transforming. The normal head of the coin was morphing into a skull. I looked at Shelly while the change was taking place. Her eyes were darkening, turning a shade of red.

"Stop," I yelled and swiped her hand. The coin fell back onto the bed. "This thing isn't right—it seems evil."

I didn't know what to do. Should I call the Swansons? It was very late, so I wasn't sure if I should wake them.

Should I call 911? Should I call Mom? Was this an emergency? It seemed like it, but I had been wrong many times before, and I needed to prove that I could do this. I could handle this.

Shelly must have been in a lot of pain. The blisters or whatever were still covering her arms. This wasn't right.

"I have to call Mom," I said.

"Are you sure it's an emergency? Her and Ed are going to be mad," Shelly replied.

I shook my head. "Who cares what Ed thinks?" I used the flashlight to reveal the path down the hall to Mom's room. I found the phone and put it to my ear, but it was dead. The phones were out, like the power. And we didn't have cell phones.

Why didn't I call sooner?

I slammed the phone in its cradle and took a deep breath, then walked back to Shelly's room. She was sitting on the bed. I patted her on the back as my stomach churned with dread. I needed to know if this only affected her or everyone else too. I didn't want those darn sores eating away at my flesh or those evil powers taking over my body. We had to know.

I got closer to the coin and felt the heat from afar. My skin shriveled at the thought of those sores attacking my body. My mind swirled. What if Shelly was stronger than me or slightly immune to the coin—could it kill me? Hot, boiling sensations charged through my chest, then up my arms and legs.

My index finger hovered over the coin, slowly getting closer and closer, until I touched it.

Thunder roared. I screamed in pain. My finger burned as if I'd grabbed a pan from a hot oven. I picked it up and passed it from hand to hand, trying to dull the heat and find out what caused it to be so dangerous.

As the coin pressed longer in my left hand, I noticed my palm turning bright red while the coin was changing. The tails side faced up and the normal eagle was being covered in a reddish, blood-like substance. It stopped flowing across the coin before it reached the glowing green edge with wavy points.

Redness covered my arms and scab-like sores flared across my hand. They rose in my palm and spread to my wrist as I held on to the coin. I switched it to my right hand and watched as the same thing happened. But, the sores on my left hand had begun to heal, though it was still red. I had never seen anything like this before.

The longer the coin was in a hand, the harder it was to move it back and forth. It almost melted into my skin. I shook my hand, but it stayed there. The pain shot up my arm and coursed through my entire body until my back bowed. Then something else attacked my body.

I felt myself wanting to change. My blood boiled, my fears disappeared. I was different. I wanted to become scary, instead of being scared.

I wanted to become evil.

"RJ!" Shelly screamed.

I threw out my arms as hard as I could, flapping like a bird. I couldn't let this coin take over my body. I stumbled into the hallway and then into the bathroom. Anxiety caused my palms to sweat, which helped loosen its hold. Then, *crack!* The coin flew off my hand and smashed into the vanity mirror.

Shelly flew after me, flashing the light on the large spider web of cracks that were etched into the mirror of the medicine cabinet. "Great! Bad luck is the last thing we need right now," she said.

She flashed the light on the coin resting in the sink. It sizzled from its recent attack, and quickly returned to a normal, harmless quarter.

I turned on the cold water to cool the coin. But the moment that the water touched it, it sizzled and transformed again. The green edges came alive in a brighter, glowing green than before. I wrenched off the water. As the coin dried, it became a normal quarter again.

I was exhausted, out of breath, spooked, and covered in sores. But then I blinked and some of them were gone, although I was still red. I couldn't figure out why the sores had disappeared. This was driving me insane. Was it because we weren't exposed to the coin long enough for all of the lesions to be permanent?

I didn't want to find out how to make these sores last a second longer than they already did. I also wasn't sure what we should do with the coin. Should we throw it out? Bury it?

"If only Mom got us those cell phones we always asked for," I said, hoping Shelly had collected something along her journeys that could help us call Mom.

"I always asked for them. You were too busy playing your video games."

"Whatever! I wanted one too. I'm probably the only twelve-year-old I know that doesn't have one." I turned and leaned against the sink while looking down at the coin, concerned about my red arms. I put my hand on my forehead, shifted my hat up, and sighed. I faced the bathroom window overlooking the front yard. As Shelly moved the flashlight, I saw something in the distance.

"Wait, what was that?" I asked.

"What was what?" She retraced where the light had been.

It was *him*, and he was approaching our
house.

—

CHAPTER EIGHT

Chills again. They invaded my body. I froze as he methodically slithered up the driveway. He'd chosen the best time to come after us. It was too late for anyone to be awake and too dark for anyone who might still be awake to see. This was a peaceful neighborhood, nothing like this ever happened here. What was different about today?

I watched in what felt like slow motion as he got closer to the door—steps away.

"What the heck is that?" Shelly asked as she caught sight of him as well.

"I don't know, but I've been seeing him ever since you ended up on thirteen's lawn. He's been everywhere, but no one else has seen him."

"What do we do? What does he want?" Shelly asked.

"He probably wants that," I said, pointing at the coin. "But we can't let him have it. Who knows what he'll do with it? Probably use it against us."

I wasn't completely sure why he was here, but it must have something to do with the coin. That had to be why he came to our lemonade stand.

What were we supposed to do? I was in charge but didn't want to be anymore. I was all done with this guy, this creature, or whatever you want to call him. It was hard enough to look at him.

Every part of my body was on edge as he went out of view, maybe approaching the front door. Anticipation was eating away at my insides. What was he going to do—break in? If only Ed hadn't gotten rid of my closet full of stuff to protect the house. Stupid Ed. It was all his fault.

Should we hide? Did he see us and know we were inside?

My head was spinning. I couldn't make a decision. I was scatterbrained and then ...

BAM ... BAM ... BAM! The door.

This time, chills raced up the back of my skull. It felt like ice. Every hair on me stood up. My body went numb. I was dizzy with panic. Shelly froze, too. If she was scared, then I had no chance.

"What do we do?" she asked.

I was terrified. I didn't have any answers. "I don't know."

"Should we open it?"

"No! Absolutely not." Was Shelly crazy? That idea hadn't even crossed my mind. We had to get out of here.

"He has to know we're in here. If we saw him, he probably saw us," she said.

I nodded. "We have to get rid of the coin. We can't let him have it." There was only one place I could think of to get rid of it.

BAM … BAM … BAM!

"Quick, grab your stuff," I ordered Shelly.

"Where are we going?" she asked.

"The lake."

"What?" Shelly was shocked. "We'd have to go through thirteen's whole backyard to get to the lake, especially if *you're* gonna throw the coin. Remember last time?"

I shrugged off her comment. "Dad disappeared there and the coin will too. It's the only way to truly get rid of it. We have to bury it at the bottom of the lake. Then all of this goes away. It has to." I lifted my arms, showing the redness that was looking permanent.

Shelly wasn't yet sold on my plan. "You've never even been on the front lawn of thirteen's property. How are you gonna get all the way to the lake? And how do you know this is gonna work? Do you see how dark it is outside?

Shelly never reacted like this. She was panting, speaking eight thousand miles per second. Her words blended together.

"It has to—unless you have a better idea?"

Shelly thought for a brief second. "What about the Swansons? They might be able to help us."

Maybe she was right. The route to the lake could be dangerous even though I knew that was the only way to really get rid of the coin. But the Swansons would hopefully know what to do or at least they could protect us from this creature, *if they believed us.*

I nodded. "Okay. Good call. Let's go to the Swansons, but we have to bring the coin."

I ran through the house, looking for something to put the coin into. I needed a safe container to prevent it from harming us. The only things upstairs that might have been useful were extra sheets and pillowcases, but with how hot Shelly's bed was, I thought something more durable would work better. Against my better judgment, I had to go downstairs to find something, probably in the kitchen—right by the front door—where The Impaler was.

Quietly and carefully, I walked through our living and dining rooms, then tiptoed into the kitchen where the door shook each time that he knocked. As I passed by it, I couldn't make out the creature's silhouette through the light blue curtain that covered the windows on the front door. Whenever anyone knocked, we could at least see their outline, but not this time—not him. Where was he hiding?

The pounding got louder and louder and the door shook harder and harder.

I reached up into the cabinets for a storage container. Mom always saved these any time we ordered take-out, so there were a million of them. I hoped that the plastic would prevent the coin's powers from activating and harming us.

I had to be quick so we could get out of here. I found a small container hidden in the back. My hand reached deeper into the cabinet until I grasped the one that I needed, then *CRASH*. They all came falling down, causing a loud noise near the door.

The knocking stopped.

Oh no, he'd definitely heard me. He had to know that I was right here.

After an agonizing few seconds, the door handle shook. He was trying to open the door. I almost lost my breath. Luckily we'd locked the deadbolt before heading upstairs. Silence. Then nothing. Where had he gone? Why would he leave if he knew we were close by? Was this a trap?

I tiptoed towards the door, trying not to make another sound in case he was still there, waiting for me to let him into the house.

Shelly came running into the kitchen, holding the coin. Her arm was blistering again, further up. I rushed the container to her so that she could put it in. I used the lid to slide the coin from her hand. She groaned in pain as new sores rose up on her arms. They weren't going away. We didn't have much time. I hoped that our skin would go back to normal once we got rid of this stupid coin.

I sealed the small plastic container, took a deep breath, and shoved it into the cargo pocket of my shorts. Then I went back toward the door to look outside, trying to see where he had gone.

I wondered if we should stay put, but also worried that he'd be back. If this thing wanted the coin, he had to know that we had it, and our parents weren't here to protect us.

I crept closer to the door, slowly, quietly. I reached out to it, barely touching it so that it didn't budge. I put my ear next to it, trying to hear anything outside. Silence. I turned and pressed my face to the window. There was nothing out in the distance. My eyes blinked, trying to focus up close, then I realized there were eyes staring back at me. He saw me.

Then a hand reached through the door and grabbed me by the neck.

CHAPTER NINE

I couldn't breathe. I was choking. Gasping.

My eyes struggled to stay open. I reached up to grab the hand that was wrapped around my neck, but I couldn't feel it to stop it. Everything around me was spinning. There was nothing I could do.

Slowly, my body went limp.

Something pulled me from behind as if I was the rope in a game of tug-o-war. But it was too late—my eyes closed and it all went black.

Cold water hit my face. My mouth flew open as the water flooded into my nose. It felt like I was going to drown.

Shelly stood above me with a pitcher, pouring water over me.

I wasn't sure how to process what had happened. Was it his hand that had grasped my throat? If so, how?

"What happened?" I struggled to ask, still rubbing my throat.

"Let's go, get up." Shelly reached her hand down to help.

We raced out of the kitchen, through the living room, to the back sunroom. There was another door there. Shelly and I had to get out of here. Otherwise, he would have us trapped and, after what had just happened, who knew what else this thing had planned for us. We had to get to the Swansons' house. We couldn't stay here.

Shelly got to the door, unlocked the dead bolt, and turned the handle. She peeked her head outside onto the porch. "Are you ready?" she asked.

I nodded, then whispered, "One ... two ... three."

Leaving the door wide open, we dashed off the porch, into our small yard, and through the grassy divide that separated our house from the Swansons' house.

Neither one of us looked back as we navigated through the dark with Shelly's flashlight. We reached the Swansons' yard and charged up the driveway and to the front door. When we got there, I pounded away—hitting the door as hard as I could. My hand felt like it was going to break off against the dense door.

We waited, hoping that the Swansons would answer in time. "Help!" I yelled. Then Shelly chimed in, yelling with me. Someone had to have heard us. Why weren't they answering?

Shelly shone the flashlight around the area, eventually pointing it back toward our house. To our dismay, he was headed this way.

I knocked harder. Time was running out. "Help, open the door, please. HELP!" I screamed and furiously kicked the door. Shelly let out an ear-splitting scream. Before today, I had never heard her scream like that. It made me more scared than I already was.

Shelly pointed her index finger toward the grassy divider between the Swansons and our house. Her finger shook like a leaf in the wind. "RJ, he's in the grass. He's here."

"Run," I yelled.

We had no choice, it was time for Plan B. Shelly and I raced to the street again, but this time we didn't head home. We couldn't yet.

We had to go to the lake.

We got to the street, and I glanced back. That was a big mistake. He was slithering right behind us through the grass. He wasn't walking with the cane anymore. It was attached to his back like a sword. He moved as if there were no bones in his body, which seemed to make him faster. He was so close that my legs picked up the pace before my brain told them to.

To reach the lake, we had to go through thirteen's yard. Never in a million years had I wanted to go onto that property. I hated that we were headed there, but we had no choice. It was our job to prevent the coin from getting into this creature's hands.

We ran as fast as we could, trying to stay in front of The Impaler. To make matters worse, rain started to fall. Drops collected on my shirt, plastering the cotton to my body. It wasn't pouring, but enough to get the grass and pavement wet. A brisk breeze picked up, and clouds quickly covered the dim crescent moon that was helping our flashlight illuminate our path.

Sweat dripped from my forehead, and my breathing was erratic. I was panting and tired, but adrenaline was kicking in.

We ran in the middle of the street, hoping that someone would see us. But because the power was out, it was too dark. We were on our own.

The leafless trees at the cul-de-sac were in front of us. We were just about there. The abandoned castle came into view. I could see the gate. I heard its rusty metal ache in the wind. I turned back to see how far behind he was. But he wasn't anywhere to be seen. My head swung forward, ready to navigate the terrain. Our flashlight flickered. "No!" I yelled, "We need that light."

Shelly shook the flashlight violently and smacked her hand against the outside of it. "If only you didn't crack the mirror. Now we're both stuck with your bad luck."

"There's no such thing," I called out, hoping I was right. We couldn't lose the flashlight. How would we know where he was? Was he waiting for us here with his cane?

Shelly didn't give up. After a few hits, the flashlight lit back up, bright again. Finally, a lucky break. She threw her arms in the air victoriously. I wished that it was that easy and this was all over. I wanted to stop and go home—to start the whole day over again and not allow him to come to our lemonade stand, or to stop Shelly from stepping foot onto this property. If only I could go back in time; I'd stop Mom from leaving us alone for the night.

No, I had to be strong. I was the older one. It was up to me to lead us to the lake and get rid of this coin.

At this point, I kept thinking about the moment that the coin would sink to the bottom of the lake. Maybe the Impaler and this house would disappear, as if the coin were his life source—like a video game. Then everything would go back to normal. We were so close, yet so far.

We reached the fence that marked the beginning of his property. It constantly creaked in the wind. I felt like it was speaking to us, saying 'go away.' The temperature felt like it dropped another ten degrees. This was it; Shelly and I were about to enter unfamiliar territory, a place that I never wanted to go. Who knew where The Impaler was now? What mattered was that we couldn't get caught. The coin had to end up in the lake.

I paused, gritted my teeth, and squinted my eyes. Reluctantly, I ducked under a broken part of the fence and my foot touched his grass. There was no turning back now.

We rushed through the yard, the lake slowly becoming visible in the distance. We looked toward the cliff's edge behind the abandoned house. It was a steep, long drop to the water, but it was doable. It had to be. But first, we had to find a way down.

"We can do this. See, I'm not afraid of everything."

"Well you might want to be afraid of that," Shelly said, pointing at The Impaler, who blocked our path.

CHAPTER TEN

Rain poured down in buckets, obscuring our view of the creature. He was here—in our way, but we had to get by. Thunder roared. We were blindly running through the yard of the scariest place in the neighborhood being chased by the scariest thing I'd ever seen.

He had to know that we were trying to dispose of the coin.

Shelly and I dove to the ground, trying to hide from him. We crawled through the wet grass like bugs until we reached a group of trees so that we could make a plan to get to the water below.

There was essentially a jungle to hike through between us and the lake. To make it worse, the yard sloped straight down until it

71

reached the edge of the cliff. I wasn't sure how we were going to get to the bottom.

Who knew what else was here with us besides him? There could be all sorts of creepy crawlers out here. Looking around, I could see a flat area down below that had been cleared. Nothing was there except fresh, smooth dirt and what appeared to be stones sticking out of the ground. Figures, it was probably a graveyard. It was below the cliff's edge, a lower tier, which I didn't know existed until now. It was eerie to look at from above. I couldn't imagine how terrifying it would be to go through it.

"Look," I reluctantly yelled over the rain while pointing to the flat ground, "we have to get there. It's our best chance to the bottom."

Shelly nodded and followed my lead.

We navigated cautiously through the grounds, fighting the rain as we went down the sloped yard. I swatted each blade of grass that flew onto my legs. I flinched. My skin crawled.

This was not me. Where was scaredy-cat RJ? Since when did I get involved with things like this? When I was with Shelly, of course. But this felt different, like it was my idea. Was I finally becoming brave? Was this what it felt like? Perhaps it was just my survival mode kicking in.

We reached another group of trees and I noticed a long tunnel that seemed to lead to the flat burial grounds. This had to be the way to get to that lower level—closer to the lake.

The tunnel looked like a laundry chute that whoever lived here probably made to send his victims to the burial grounds. Shelly and I poked our heads into it and looked down. I took the flashlight, shining it into the tunnel and moving it around, trying to figure out what this was used for. It appeared to be made of a strong plastic that was dug into the ground, but it was tough to tell.

"Do you want to go first?" I asked Shelly, hoping she'd take the bait.

"You go, I'll slide down after you." She stepped out of the way so I could get in position.

Flying fishsticks, that wasn't the answer I wanted to hear. Sure, I was older and should protect her, but she loved this stuff, lived for it. I figured she would have been all about going first.

I sat at the entrance of the tunnel and listened to the rain pound on the top of it. The sound echoed. It was so loud that it felt like the tunnel could cave in at any moment and crush me. I stared through it, noticing how long and scary it was. My eyes were playing tricks on me as the walls appeared to be closing in. Was I claustrophobic? Maybe this wasn't the best idea, perhaps there was another way. There had to be. I tried to get to my feet and get out of this trap, but a pair of hands pushed me.

"No," I yelled as I flew down the slide. "Shelly!" My voice echoed in the tunnel. Did she really push me? I would never have done that to her.

My butt barely touched the tube as my speed constantly increased. *Yup, I'm definitely claustrophobic—add that to the list. I need air.*

In an attempt to settle my anxiety, I closed my eyes, hoping that I'd be able to escape. My body shook from left to right while speeding down the slide.

Closing my eyes wasn't any better. *I feel like I'm gonna puke.* I thought.

Finally, I collided with the smooth dirt. My head felt woozy and I struggled with the pain from the hard collision, but I was so glad to be out of there. The flashlight had fallen out of my hands and was spinning on the ground, then it stopped, shining the light on the burial grounds.

I rubbed my head, shifted around quickly, and tried to pull myself up, but my left leg wouldn't move. It felt like it was on fire. I reached down and grabbed at it, wondering if there was a cut or bruise from the tunnel. I grabbed the flashlight and shined it on me. Both of my legs were bright red.

The pain got worse. So bad that I had to fight the urge to scream my head off. What was happening? Was I being stung? That was what it felt like—a bee sting that wouldn't stop.

I lifted up the leg of my wet cargo shorts. Mud had smeared against my skin. I pushed the shorts leg up and found the tender spot. It was on the outside of my leg, above my knee.

Sores popped up on my leg. *The coin.*

I stuck my hand into my pocket, feeling for the container, but it wasn't there. I searched the area trying to find it, but it was gone.

Digging deeper into my pocket made me realize that the coin had shifted around and eaten through the plastic. It was about to do the same to my leg. The pocket of my shorts glowed green. Evil flooded my body. Dreadful thoughts of death and destruction swarmed my mind— things that would normally have me hiding under my bed. It was attacking my body like a fast-acting stomach bug. I wanted to puke the evil out of me to feel better.

My hand scrambled to find the coin. When I grasped it from inside my pocket, I threw it into the wet dirt, and struggled to my feet. The wound repaired itself instantly and the terrible thoughts disappeared from my mind.

I shined the light so I could look through to the top of the tube, trying to locate Shelly. I was going to yell at her for pushing me, but the rain and darkness made it difficult to see. Something didn't feel right. Was it actually Shelly who pushed me?

My yell echoed in the tube, but she didn't respond. Then I caught a glimpse of Shelly. The creature had my sister in his grasp. She had nowhere to go.

Without thinking, I ducked my head and ran up the tunnel. I was going to do my best to get back up there and save her. There was no time to be typical RJ right now—I had to be brave RJ.

As my feet climbed into the beginning of the tunnel, I called out for Shelly, but my feet quickly lost traction. I slipped and my face smashed into the ground. My own voice taunted me as the sound of my yelling was trapped in the tunnel, echoing back to me. There was no way that I could get up this way. What was I supposed to do?

"RJ! RJ!" Shelly yelled, then her voice became muffled, tapered off, and was gone.

Her cries repeated inside my head. I was helpless to save her. Mom left me in charge, and it was unclear if I'd ever see my sister again.

I looked around, hoping for a clue—a way back up—but there was nothing. No other secret passageways were visible.

My eyes darted to the lake then down at the coin. I had to throw the coin in the water to save Shelly, but that would require me getting to the bottom of this cliff or mountain, or whatever it was. Otherwise, I wasn't sure that the coin would end up in the lake.

Looking down at the coin, I cursed at it in my own head with every bad word I knew. Why did it come into my life? I checked out my arms and legs, which were so red, and I couldn't help but wonder, how much worse was this going to get?

I wanted all of this to be over. I wasn't the adventurous type. There wasn't any part of me that wanted to climb down the rest of this cliff to drop the coin in the lake. I'd rather be at home in my room, reading or playing video games about someone else who had to do it, someone like Shelly. She would have been perfect for this job. I wished that I'd been the one that had gotten captured because she would have been able to do this with ease. But not me.

Somehow, I had to channel my inner Shelly. We were brother and sister, so there had to be some of her fearlessness inside me, didn't there? But maybe that wasn't enough.

All of my fears needed to go away. I had to find a way to forget about all the things I worried about. There was only one way I could think of that would make me completely fearless.

I had to become evil.

CHAPTER ELEVEN

I was filled with determination as I peered down at the lake. Nothing was going to stop me from getting the coin in that water and saving Shelly. I was sick of worrying. She needed me, and I was going to come through.

I had to use the powers of the coin to help me no matter what the consequences were. It was still unclear how this thing worked, but I never felt as strong as I did when I had it in my hands. Though, I knew the longer it was in my possession, the more evil my body felt. Hopefully, it wouldn't change me forever.

I wiped the mud from my hands against my shirt, leaving wet prints. I reached for the coin. *This was going to burn,* I thought. I could deal with the consequences later—anything to save Shelly.

I looked at the coin, cursed it once more, and then held onto it, ready to accept its power.

Evil rushed through my veins. It was scary how easily this coin changed the way I thought and felt. Feelings of fiery heat attacked my body. Thoughts of doom and gloom filled my brain. I screamed in pain. It felt like I was being struck by lightning. My fists clenched and my arms extended. I felt the need to pound my chest like a gorilla. I was losing control. My hands grabbed at the collar of my shirt and ripped it away.

Rain poured onto my husky torso, which seemed bigger, as if I was being pumped full of evil. My whole body was itchy, sore, and red. Normally, I would have been instantly chilled by the rain, instead I barely felt the drops pounding against my body. I was powerful—immune to everything around me.

My anxiety vanished. I felt different. My eyes adjusted to the darkness—like I had night vision goggles on. Without thinking, I jammed the flashlight in my cargo pocket and bolted toward the lake like an agile cat. Out of the corner of my eye, the stones from the burial ground came into view. I didn't stop to check them out, even though there might have been ones with Shelly's and my names on them. I didn't think about that though. Instead, I found myself thinking of who *should* end up in that graveyard. Those bullies from school wouldn't mess with me if I had this kind of power and if they did, that was where they'd go. And if I could find out who was responsible for my dad's death, they'd go there too.

These sinister thoughts were spine chilling to the old, scaredy-cat RJ. But to me, the opposite, evil RJ—JR—or whatever I was becoming, they were thrilling, exhilarating. Was this why people wanted to be evil?

I moved as fast as I could, traversing the rainy terrain. It was slippery, but my shoes gripped with glue-like precision. It was as if I were Shelly. This was how I'd picture her getting down the rest of this area. *Shelly? I was forgetting my mission. Why was I here?*

Wet leaves, left over from autumn, squashed underneath my feet. Everything blurred past until I neared the edge of the cliff. *What was I doing? Where was I headed?*

Trying to stop, I lost my balance.

I slipped, fell, and the coin flew out of my hand, landing in the leaves around me. I splashed onto the ground and slid toward the edge. I dug my toes in to the mud, trying to slow down. I reached my arms out, grabbing for anything, until I caught hold of a rope. A rope! My hands fumbled with it. Frantically, I kept scraping for it and was able to grab hold as my body swung over the edge of the cliff.

Oh no, this is it. I'm going to fly off the edge and end up dead.

My hands held tight while I dangled off the cliff. I looked down. Luckily it was too dark to really see how far it was, but I heard small rocks fall off the cliff and it seemed to take forever to hit the ground. Nausea flooded my stomach and my fingers burned, ready to let go any second now and send me plummeting twenty or thirty feet to the ground.

My anxiety was back, taking the place of the evil that was seeping out of me. I slowed my rapid breathing and tried to swing my legs up. I was desperate for solid ground. It took a few attempts and a lot of struggling, but I was able to pull myself onto the grassy ledge, where I collapsed. Every part of me ached.

I lay in the mud with rain falling on me, wondering how I got into this mess. Instinctively, I thought of the coin.

Wait—where was the coin? It was gone. I sat up and dug in the leaves around me. I took the flashlight out of my pocket and shined it around me, but I didn't see the coin anywhere. Frantically, I searched the whole area. What was I going to do? Without it, I wouldn't be able to get the coin to the bottom of the lake so all of this madness would stop.

I watched the rain collect in puddles on the soaked leaves. Sizzling filled the air and the leaves glowed green.

The coin.

Before I grabbed it again, I needed a plan. I shined the flashlight all around. Above me was the upper cliff, with the tunnel that brought me here. To my left and right were more woods, but there wasn't any other way down to the very bottom except for the rope. It was still too far to throw the coin from here because I wasn't directly above the water. Once I got to the bottom of this drop off, I could run to the lake's shoreline. Then, like in all of my video games, I'd get the coin in the lake and finish the job, then the game would be over. Too bad it wasn't just a game, this was much more serious.

I was fixated on the rope. As far as I could tell, there were no stairs or other way down, except for the rope. It appeared that was my only option, unless I'd missed something.

I couldn't climb all the way back up. There was no time and I didn't know how to. Besides, I didn't know what was happening to Shelly. She could be imprisoned and being tortured by The Impaler.

I looked over the edge one more time and took a deep breath to settle the dizzy feeling that swept my senses. This was it. I was going to have to conquer my fear of heights and get to the bottom of this cliff. Cautiously, I walked to the edge and grabbed for the rope that hung from a large tree nearby. Reaching over the edge, I pulled more slack rope up so that I could test how strong it was. I wasn't sure when anyone used this last, but this was my only chance to get down to the water.

Tugging on the rope made me feel slightly better as it seemed strong. Maybe this wouldn't be so bad. In my head, I pictured gliding down the rope nice and slowly. *That'd be perfect. I'd end up in the grass, run to the water, throw the coin, and all of this would be over. Easy.*

This all sounded great to me. Well, kind of. I don't know if 'great' was the right word, but ending all of this would be. However, I knew that none of this would be possible without the coin.

I turned around and found it again. I put the flashlight into my pocket and reached down for the coin. I grabbed it. Instantly, I was overcome by the powers again.

Fearlessly, I grabbed the rope and started my descent down the side of this cliff. My hands gripped it tightly, and my feet used the cliff to rappel down. This was as easy as I thought it would be.

I was making quick work of the cliff. Maybe too quick because as I was ten feet or so from the grassy shore, the rope jerked. My eyes shot up to the tree, which was shaking. The rope was starting to fray. It wasn't going to hold me much longer.

My legs pushed off the cliff harder and harder, until about six feet above the ground, the rope gave way. Next, came the tree.

Timber! The tree was starting its collapse over the edge and was aiming right at me. I was headed for the ground, back first, and had no idea what I was about to land on.

My arms reacted on their own, swimming through the air as if they could slow me down. They reached for something, anything, to grab, but instead, the coin flew out of my hand.

Wham—thud! I hit the ground like an asteroid making impact with the earth's surface. Pain shot through my entire body. The coin landed on my chest, just missing my heart. Instantly, my skin singed, like I was being branded. Before I could rip the coin away, I flung my arms over my face as pieces of the tree crashed on top of me.

"Augh," I yelled. The tree crashed into the ground, next to me, breaking into a million pieces. A dust cloud of splinters and wood flew at me, jabbing into my arms and legs. But they didn't hurt as much as they should have. I was too focused on the pain from my chest.

My heart beat faster and harder until I reached up and pulled the coin from my chest.

Its evil skull had etched into my body like a tattoo, but that didn't matter. I was breathing. I'd made it.

I shot to my feet, holding the coin, then sprinted until water touched my sneakers. They squished into the muddy shore. It was time to throw the coin.

Sharp screams punctuated the air behind me. It sounded like Shelly — unless The Impaler had captured someone else. It had to be her. I had to ignore it — the coin had to go. Plus, I didn't want to end up evil from all of the toxic power rushing through me. Luckily, I was able to keep most of my own consciousness. I had come this far and I had to finish the job to end all of the madness.

I took the coin into my right hand, raised my arm, cocked it back, then hurled it as far as I could. I watched the trajectory and waited for the splash. The coin crashed into the water and sent massive ripples roaring through the lake. It looked like a nuclear bomb had exploded miles below the surface. But it was done. The coin was gone. I collapsed to my knees. My whole body tensed. I was now covered from head to toe in sores. Yes, even my face. I could feel them. This had to work, I couldn't stay like this.

I turned my shoulders and faced the house, then looked up. Shelly was still with The

Impaler, and she was screaming something at the top of her lungs.

Bubbling sounds came from the lake. I turned and watched the water boil. Was this the end of everything? How it would all go back to normal? The coin would melt. The Impaler would disappear into thin air, and we would wake up back in time before the lemonade stand ever happened? Yes, I thought, that was exactly what would happen.

Instead, I watched as more and more bubbles formed on the surface of the lake. The water was turning red, like the tails' side of the coin. Something was happening. Loud screams from below the water bombarded my eardrums—they sounded like lobsters being boiled alive. This wasn't good.

As I reached up to cover my ears, one of the biggest fish I'd ever seen shot about ten feet out of the water and fell back down, floating on the surface.

The coin was attacking the lake. Everything I'd thought had been wrong.

CHAPTER TWELVE

I was in shock—defeated. Every last bit of
determination had been sucked out of my body.
How would I ever save Shelly now?

I collapsed to the ground and clutched my
head. How had this not worked? I screamed in
frustration while staring at the hazardous lake.
I grabbed a handful of rocks from the shoreline
and threw them, bellowing angrily.

I was in complete disbelief. I'd really
thought that the coin would disappear into the
lake like Dad did and all of this would be over.

What else was there left to do? Offer myself
up as a trade for Shelly? Hopefully, The Impaler
would be willing to keep me instead and let my
sister go.

Suddenly, I could hear something walking
toward me. Footsteps got louder through the

darkness. This was it. I didn't have it in me to pull out the flashlight again. It was over. He was here for me. I wasn't even going to be able to propose the trade because he was about to have both of us.

Bam! Something stabbed through the shoreline right next to my hand. It lit up the area with a reddish tint. I looked over—it was the cane. The eyes from the skull at the top of it beamed a dark red light. My heart sank.

Slowly, I lifted my head. My sister was standing over me, holding the cane. I jumped up and hugged her like never before, squeezing as tight as I could until she coughed and tried to talk. I was so glad to have her back.

Shelly gasped at the sight of me. "He was right," she said.

"Who? How?" I tried to ask, pulling away from her, while pointing at the cane. "What did you do to him? It worked?" I danced like a little kid without a care in the world—so proud of my efforts.

Shelly stared at me, waiting for me to finish. "Not exactly."

"What? How did you get away?"

"He's trying to help us," Shelly said.

No way, that was the most ridiculous thing I had ever heard. We'd literally nearly died running away from him. How was he helping? I looked at her in disbelief, wondering if he had somehow brainwashed her. Was this really Shelly? Did he trick her? "What do you mean?"

"He knows about the coin."

"Of course," I said. "He wants its power. That thing's evil. Trust me."

"No, he's drawn to it. That's why he came to our lemonade stand. He knew this would happen to you. Someone else is after us," Shelly said.

"I didn't see anyone else chasing us." I pointed around the area then tilted my head, trying to process what she was telling me.

"Quick, come with me. Talk to him. We're running out of time," she urged.

This was unbelievable. We had the perfect opportunity to run away. I had Shelly back. We could go home and try to forget all of this. We could move on, act like none of this had ever happened. But then I looked at my sister and the trust in her eyes. She was convinced that The Impaler was trying to help us. As crazy as it seemed, I believed her.

Shelly walked toward the base of the cliff. I groaned, but followed close behind. I looked up and saw the outline of the monstrous castle. From down here it was like a skyscraper—like the Statue of Liberty. How were we going to get in? There was no chance that we'd be able to go back up. Even the rope was gone.

"How are we going to get inside?" I asked, catching up to Shelly, who was picking up speed as she walked toward the cliff.

"I have the key."

"Where?"

Shelly ignored my question and reached out to the side of the cliff, feeling for something. She pushed against the rock with all of her might. Nothing happened.

"What are you doing? That's solid," I said, touching the same area that she was pressing against.

Shelly kept moving her hands across the area, pushing harder on each new place she touched. Still nothing. It was useless. Why were we doing this?

"Maybe we should go, Shell?" I couldn't help but suggest. Perhaps I had been deceived too. Maybe all of this was nonsense and she was hoping for the best. It might be time to quit and get out of here as fast as possible.

Shelly refused to respond to my notion. She ripped off a chunk of the cliff, like it was starting to crumble. Rumbling filled the air, then dirt fell from the cliff as it moved.

Oh no! The cliff was collapsing inward. I crouched, closed my eyes, and covered my head, waiting for it all to topple on us. This wasn't the way. Why would this be the way in? What a terrible way to die—by being buried alive, especially after coming this far. I had really thought we were going to make it.

Shelly's obnoxious cackle stopped my incessant thoughts of death. I opened my eyes and looked up at her. She was pointing at me, while laughing at my fear. Then she took the cane and pressed the sharp edge into a slot in the cliff. *That's what his cane was for; a secret entrance.*

We walked inside and saw another door. Shelly inserted the cane into the keyhole. A bolt unlocked and she pushed it open. It was dark inside, but the red glowing eyes of the cane gave off enough light to be able to tell that we were at the entrance to the lower level of the castle. There was no turning back.

As we walked, my eyes shot through the darkness each time I heard a sound. My nerves were getting the best of me. My anxiety was on high alert. Code Red. This was my worst nightmare—a weird haunted house, some creature after us, and whatever else was here.

We entered a long hallway. Small fire lanterns lined the outside of the wall that led us into a large lit up room, which appeared to be the library. There were so many books. Some were scattered across the floor, while others filled the floor-to-ceiling shelves. Wasn't this always the case with creepy places? Books everywhere?

I looked around, mesmerized by the sheer size of the room and the height of the ceilings. I couldn't imagine how big the whole house was. There had to be hundreds of rooms. Then I heard the screeching sound. *Shrieeeeek.* The hairs on my neck stood up.

It was Shelly, she had scratched the cane against the floor. I shot her a look. But she pointed the cane toward the other doorway. It was him. He was here.

"H-hi," I stammered.

The creature stood there. He was covered as usual from head to toe. He wore his large hat, the mask that covered his face, his long black trench coat, cut-off red gloves, black pants, and his boots with metal straps. Somehow, he was even scarier inside this house.

The Impaler's eyes pierced my soul. He swam around the room, circling me like a shark. He hadn't said a word yet. It was like a dog getting a human's scent—testing the waters to see if I was trustworthy.

"Stay still," The Impaler said.

I must have turned white. This was the first time I heard him talk. His voice was like nothing I'd ever heard come out of a human being. It was robot-like but deep and dark, and it echoed throughout the library. Everything about this guy was scary. For some reason I had hoped that he'd have a high-pitched squeal for a voice, but nothing about today was going as planned.

I didn't move—I even held my breath. He reached out and took the cane from Shelly, then he held the cane against my chest, where the skull was imprinted on my body. Was he going to stab his cane through me?

I felt a small sizzle and winced, struggling to hold still. But I was paralyzed at this point. The cane caused the outline of the skull to turn green, then red, then disappear. Next, all of the sores were sucked back into my skin. Everything was gone.

"He did the same for me," Shelly said, holding out her arms which were sore-free also.

The Impaler pulled the cane away from my chest. What had just happened? All I knew was that I wouldn't have to explain the burn mark that looked like a tattoo to my mom the next time we went to the pool. I thanked him numerous times. He barely nodded and approached the long conference table in the middle of the room. There were a few books arranged on it.

"Who are you?" I asked in awe of what he had done for my chest.

The Impaler ignored my question and sat down at the head of the table. He motioned for me and Shelly to join him and we did. A black and white binder sat in front of him. He slid it to me. I reached out, grabbed the book, and quickly opened it. The first words I saw were "Project: FrightVision."

I kept reading. This was a book of experiments that had taken place in the eighties and nineties. It appeared that the scientists were scaring kids and using the fear that their bodies produced to create "unspeakable evil." Those words alone created an earthquake within my body. I could feel my heart spasm.

Nervously, I flipped through the pages, quickly scanning them. There were pictures of kids and random objects, with different experiment results on each page. Cameras, cell phones, test tubes, lamps, pens, books, clothes, toys, retainers, toothbrushes, all sorts of things were paired with different kids. It didn't make sense.

Then, as I was still going through the book, The Impaler reached over and stopped me from moving onto another page. I stopped there and looked at what he was showing me. "Specimen 1849." On the right was a picture of a young boy, photographed from an instant film camera. He looked terrified. Underneath the photo was more information about the boy. He was 12 years old and afraid of snakes, spiders, and drowning. There was also a list of the experiments that he went through. It looked like there had been twelve experiments, with the last one taking place in August of 1992 in "The Nightmare Room."

"Whoa!" Shelly said, pointing to the picture at the bottom of the page. It was of the coin with a caption, *see page 74*. "That's it," I yelled, flipping the pages to find number seventy-four.

There it was, another picture of the coin from both the front and back stapled onto the page. Below it, were headlines in bold: How Created, Powers, Most Powerful, and Least Powerful. It was created because of Patient 1849. They used the power of that kid's fears to create this evil coin!

My eyes locked on the page. It was tough to focus as I read about the coin's powers. Obviously the sores were caused by the coin and it could alter a human's mindset. But then I gasped as I read more. The coin could turn *anyone* who was exposed to it evil, no matter how little the time of exposure, and its effects were eventually permanent.

I didn't still feel evil. Was I going to change? Forever? "What is all of this?" I yelled out.

Methodically, The Impaler moved his hands to his head. Slowly, he took off his hat and placed it on the table. His hair was knotted and patchy. His flaky scalp was red with many bald spots. The plastic mask that covered his face was fully revealed. His head was smaller than I expected — it seemed like he wasn't fully grown.

Still, only his eyes and scaly lips were visible through the mask. Each part of this process left me frozen. I couldn't turn away. I looked into his eyes.

He turned his back to us, took off his coat, and dropped it on the floor. He wore a sleeveless black shirt, a black choker collar, and black pants. I noticed that he was standing on something. Stilts. That was why he was so tall. He wasn't an old creepy man, he was young—a kid about my age. He stepped down from the stilts as he turned toward us. The Impaler was about as tall as I was. Then he removed his gloves, one by one. His hands were bright red. They were scarred worse than anything I'd ever seen before. Lastly, he lifted the mask over his head. I gasped at the sight of his face.

The sores that Shelly had woken up with earlier covered The Impaler's face. They were dried, but looked painful.

"No way," Shelly said.

"You're just a kid," I said.

"I *was* just a kid," The Impaler said as he reached up to the collar around his neck. He took it off. I realized that it was a box that changed the sound of his voice. Once he removed it, he sounded like an ordinary young boy, but with pain in his voice.

"Why won't your sores go away? Can I put your cane to your body?" I asked him.

"The coin. And no. It's too late for me," The Impaler replied in his normal, high pitched voice, which was a lot less scary.

"Why?"

"I was used as part of an experiment." He bowed his head, trying to hide the way that he looked. "I'm the reason why the coin exists."

"The experiments from the book?" I was horrified that anyone could do this to a kid.

The Impaler lifted his shirt, revealing his lower back. Branded into his skin was 1849.

"You're patient 1849? You created the coin?"

"There are a group of scientists doing terrible things. They get their power from kids' fears. They use the power for evil. The tests they did caused all of this." The Impaler pointed to his sores and scars. "I couldn't fight off the evil that was constantly attacking my body. It was torture."

"Who? Where?" Were we in danger now, too?

The Impaler reached his arms out, then up, as if he was referring to this house. Then he walked closer to us. "I don't sense the evil on you anymore."

"What do you mean?" I asked.

"The evil is gone. It's attacking something else." The Impaler got close to me and scanned my body. "Where's the coin?" The Impaler kept getting closer, invading my personal bubble.

"I threw it in the lake. I—" I started to say, backing away.

"What?" He slammed his fist on the table.

"I—I—I'm sorry. I thought it would end all of this." I begged for forgiveness. Even though the Impaler was my size and age, he was still intimidating.

"I knew the lake was a bad idea," Shelly said, shaking her head.

"No you didn't," I said to her.

The Impaler stepped back and said, "We need the coin. The evil will attack the lake and everything in it."

"I felt it. I used its powers to get through the backyard and to the lake," I said.

"You've been touched by the coin." The Impaler stared deep into my soul. "You resisted its powers?"

"I used them to make me stronger. I had to. It was the only way to save her," I said, pointing at Shelly, who shifted in her shoes.

"That must be why you were targeted and so covered in sores. Your power is strong," The Impaler said as he sat back down. "There will be others that come after you, just like they did me. I was captured and taken from my family. Everything went black and I ended up in a cell, clamped down, with nowhere to go. I can't remember anything else."

"By who?" I asked.

"The scientists. Whoever they are ... they used the coin to find you." Then The Impaler whispered, while looking me in the eyes with his freaky stare, "they want your fear."

Waves of chills shot through my body as I processed what he was saying. All of this was crazy—how was this real life?

"I'm sorry for chasing and scaring you. That wasn't my intention. But when the coin's powers were activated, the evil attacked my body. I always know when someone is using it. Electricity attacks my body."

I couldn't believe it.

"Whoever left this for you has to be nearby. Maybe even part of the neighborhood," The Impaler said.

"No way." I crossed my arms, refusing to believe that someone had specifically chosen me and Shelly. *Who are we and why would anyone want us?*

The Impaler tilted his head. "Didn't you just experience the powers of the cursed coin? Isn't it out there attacking the lake as we speak?" He creased his brow.

"Why us? This can't be real. It must be a dream—a nightmare."

Shelly stood silent, but it was unclear whose side she was on. Did she believe The Impaler, or was she agreeing with me?

"There are plenty of nightmares here, but this is not one of them," The Impaler said, extending his arms, implying that the scares were everywhere in this house. "We must stop the coin … we're running out of time."

"Not until we know for sure. I'm not risking our lives anymore until we know that we're doing the right thing." Somehow, I stood up to the Impaler.

"You feeling okay?" Shelly whispered to me.

Whoa, I thought to myself. *Where did that come from? Shelly must be rubbing off on me.*

"It's not safe, but if you want evidence then I will show you some." The Impaler motioned for us to follow him down the long hallway that he came in from. He was going to take us deeper into the house. I wanted proof, but was I ready for what he was about to show us?

CHAPTER THIRTEEN

The inside of the supposed abandoned house was dark, barely lit, but The Impaler's cane helped light our way more in a reddish, eerie kind of way. The hallway continued on forever. There were closed cell-like doors on each side of us as we walked.

"What are those?" Bars made an X on the small windows in the cement doors, making it difficult to know what was behind them.

"Shhhhhh. Quiet." The Impaler replied. "You mustn't draw attention. They are here." He pointed toward the ceiling as we all stopped.

We listened intently, waiting for a sound.

Footsteps clanked above us.

"Did you hear that?" Shelly whispered.

I nodded. He was right. There was someone else here. But who?

The Impaler pressed a single finger to his lips. Slowly, he proceeded down the hallway, passing door after door, until he stopped at one on the left. He took his cane and slid the sharp end into the slot in the door.

Quietly, The Impaler pushed open the cell door.

It was as terrible and cold as I could have imagined. The air smelt damp, kind of dirty too, like a boys' locker room. The cell was a small confined area, one that had caused The Impaler to stop. His head rapidly moved and his eyes darted around the room like he saw something.

He looked lost; vacant behind those young eyes. Sad even. My mouth opened, ready to ask him if he was okay. Then loud cries for help echoed through the cement walls. The cries sounded young.

My face numbed. I reached up and pinched my cheeks, making sure I still had feeling in them. I wasn't sure what I was experiencing. Why hadn't I just believed The Impaler, instead of making him prove himself?

The Impaler looked at Shelly, then me. "This was my cell," he whispered. His head turned quickly to the left. "There. Do you see that?" he asked, pointing to the dark wall.

There was nothing. I squinted, trying to will something to appear so that The Impaler didn't seem crazy. "See what?"

"The spiders."

I jumped back, fearful that I was about to be attacked by a cluster of tarantulas. Shelly held her ground, this was probably right up her alley. She would probably try to take one home.

I fell back against the cell door, my eyes fixed on the wall. But no spiders appeared. I only saw a small square in the wall. It looked like a brick was missing. Near the hole was something glowing in the dark—a fisherman's lure—just like the one my dad and I used when we went fishing.

Huh? Why would that be here?

"There ..." He interrupted my thoughts, pointing toward another part of the wall.

Shelly and I turned our heads.

"Snakes," The Impaler called out.

Now I wanted to scream. My whole body felt like it was going through a washing machine. Up. Down. Back. Forth. I was drowning in anxiety. The pressure against my chest was intense. It was worse because I couldn't see what he saw, yet his eyes were mesmerized. He wasn't joking with us.

Shelly shifted closer to me. Our arms touched. She looked a little freaked out by The Impaler's reactions. But to us, nothing was here. What did they do to him in this cell?

Suddenly, I could feel things crawling across my body. They had to exist only in my mind, didn't they?

"Do you see it—any of it?" The Impaler asked, breaking his intense stare.

I shook my head as Shelly responded, "No, nothing."

Despair, sadness, and loneliness seemed to strike The Impaler all at once. It looked like he wanted to collapse and never get up. "I need to get out of this cell. I can't do this again, but there's more to see." He motioned for us to follow.

After we all exited the cell, he closed the door carefully. The Impaler signaled for us to continue and we did, until we reached the final door. It was directly in front of us, and there was nowhere further to go. We were far away from the library at this point. It felt like we had been walking for twenty minutes and it all led to this spot. The last door. What was behind it?

CHAPTER FOURTEEN

What was this place that we were trying to enter? Did I still need proof that The Impaler was telling the truth? There was obviously something weird going on around here. Why did I need to see more?

The footsteps above us got louder. There was some loud grumbling. Then, *smash*, something hit the floor above us, sounding like whatever it was shattered everywhere.

My stomach sank. I was done with this place—ready to get the heck out of here. I turned my head around, desperate to see the library—begging to know the way out of here in case we needed to run. But it was pitch black and my eyes refused to adjust to the lack of light. Nothingness. What was going to happen to us? Were we going to make it out of here alive?

Once again, The Impaler used his cane to unlock the door, but it wouldn't open. The door wouldn't budge.

Shelly groaned as she pushed against the door with all her might. I looked around, wondering when whoever was above us was going to appear. There were no stairs. At least we didn't come across any—none that I saw anyway. How were you supposed to get up to the top floor of this castle?

"There," The Impaler said as he pointed out a second slot that needed to be unlocked. He handed Shelly a skeleton key from his pocket. She reached up and inserted it into the slot, then a red button lit up above the keyhole. This was it, all she had to do was press it.

Shelly slammed her hand into it and the door slid open to the left. "Got it!"

We were in. Sort of.

Plastic sheets hung from floor-to-ceiling, blocking our view of the room. Cautiously, we pushed them aside and entered.

What … the heck … was that?

I crossed my arms and backed away, nearly falling out of the room through the plastic. I had never seen anything like this before. There was a clear box in the middle of the room, about waist high. It sat on a tall black pedestal, like a metal pole. Behind that, a chair was bolted to the ground. Black and red wires hung from the box as if they were jumper cables ready to start a car, but judging from what The Impaler said about the scientists, I doubted they were used for that.

"Whoa," said Shelly.

A laptop was set up next to the stand, which was also connected to the box. It too was on a pedestal, this one much larger with a lot of room underneath it. There was also a stool for someone to sit at to operate the computer. Nothing was on the screen.

Slowly, I looked closer at the clear box. There was something in it. Something odd … squirmy … pink … alive.

My legs walked toward it. My mind was shut off—overloaded—hopefully restarting. I kept walking closer, looking harder, and finally, stood above the box.

Holy flying fishsticks! I yelled in my head so loud that it woke my mind up.

It was a brain—a human one. *Whose was it? One of the kids from inside this place? Were there more or was it just The Impaler?*

My lips parted, ready to yell as loud as possible. A hand quickly covered my mouth before I let loose the loudest scream on planet Earth. I was muted in the nick of time, but I lost my balance.

Stumbling backwards, I tried to regain my footing, but I was going down. Reaching out, I tried to catch my balance. Instead, I grabbed the computer station, nearly taking it down with me, but my hand slid off.

Time felt as if it stopped as I was frozen in mid-air. My eyes darted around, hoping that there would be something to cushion my fall. But nothing came into view.

"RJ!" Shelly yelled.

I landed hard on cold cement, crashing into a wooden crate, which broke into pieces. Though there was nothing in it, the damage was the sound it made when it exploded. Like someone taking a sledgehammer to the wall.

Footsteps thundered above us. I could tell by how loud the steps were that there was more than one set.

A bright green light flashed in the far corner of the room, in the shape of a down arrow. It was marking an elevator. Whoever was on the floor above was on their way to find us.

"Quick!" The Impaler shouted, ignoring his previous requests for quiet, as he rushed to the door. He slammed the cane into the first slot, but he needed the key for the other one.

Shelly reached back into her pocket, her hands shaking violently as she fumbled for the key.

Now! Quick! I thought. We had to get out of here. I believed The Impaler. There was nothing else that I needed to see to know that he was telling the truth. This place was a madhouse. Who knew it was in our quiet neighborhood?

Finally, Shelly got hold of the key and reached for the second slot.

The elevator beeped.

The door opened.

We dove to the ground and scurried out of sight.

Out walked two older men dressed in long, white lab coats. Their eyes darted around the room as they approached the brain. "Everything seems to be okay here," one man said.

"Over there," the other guy pointed at the broken crate.

"Must've fallen from the desk."

They both nodded as we crouched behind a bookcase that hung like a shelf in the corner of the room. We had grabbed as many pieces of the crate as we could and used them as a shield to help us stay hidden. One move and they would spot us and we'd be dead. We had to be quiet. Then I looked towards the door.

The key was still hanging from the second slot. Hopefully, they wouldn't notice.

One of the scientists walked around the room as if he were a bloodhound hot on the trail of something. Did he see the key? Was there something else that we left behind?

The scientist walked toward the door. *Oh no … he's going to see the key.* If he did, they'd know that someone was in here. *Please, don't look at the door. Please.*

Beep. The elevator opened and the lurking scientist stopped before he got to the door. He turned and walked back to the elevator.

"He's ready," said a new man, who appeared to be a security guard. He was dressed in all black with a nightstick and a taser. He was holding someone hostage, dragging them into the room. I couldn't really tell who or what yet because my view was blocked.

"Take off the gag," a scientist said.

A tearing sound roared through the room.

"Help. No. Please. Not the nightmare room!"

The cries were coming from a shrieking kid. Yes a boy, who sounded about my age. Who were these people and what were they going to do?

There was a massive struggle between the scientists and the kid, who was kicking and screaming. The boy stopped yelling. They must've gagged him again.

I inched up on one knee. We had to help. Didn't we?

The Impaler reached out, holding me down. It was as if he knew I wanted to run out there and save the kid. He shook his head.

My view was much better now that I was kneeling. I could see the kid. He was a boy, *one that I knew—Johnny!*

The scientists had dressed him in a bright yellow jumpsuit, and he was gagged again with shiny black tape. They must have grabbed him when the three boys went to the house while we sold lemonade. No wonder the other boys rode away as fast as possible. But why didn't they say anything? How was he captured?

The scientists forcefully slammed Johnny into the chair and strapped him down. Once he was in position, they put a pair of virtual reality goggles over his eyes, then said, "Let's begin."

Begin what? What didn't they want him to see? Or worse yet, what *did* they want him to see?

One scientist reached for the wires that were connected to the brain. The black one went to the red knob on the goggles, and the red one went to the black knob.

Jolts of electricity filled the room. Lights flickered. It was as if they actually were jumpstarting a human being instead of a car. We were all nearly blown back to the walls as this transfer of power took place. The shelves shook.

Johnny's hair stood up on end. I could tell he was trying to scream as his cheeks tensed until the tape couldn't hold him back anymore. The adhesive flew off his mouth and his piercing scream nearly put a hole in my body.

"No ... not a rat! No!" Johnny yelled.

Instinctively, I looked around the room, trying to find a rodent, but there weren't any to be found. But, I bumped the bookshelf. It waivered. We reached out and steadied it.

Vibrations from the center of the room masked any noise from the shaking shelves. I looked toward the box with the brain, which rocked violently back and forth. Was there a rat or something in the container?

I squinted, trying to figure out what was happening. No rat. The brain moved by itself. Shook. The power from the kid must have been fueling it. Then ooze shot across the room, splattering against the wall, nearly catching me in the face. The brain just about split open. Something was about to crawl out of it.

CHAPTER FIFTEEN

Volts of electricity from the cables hooked to Johnny baked the room. The temperature went up about twenty degrees as the machine began overheating.

I covered my eyes with the brim of my hat. I couldn't watch.

As I leaned my head back, my hat slowly shifted off my eyes, and the brain was in my sight. Black as night, sharp nails inched their way out of the oozing, separating brain.

Next came pale blue fingers, which bent, then extended methodically as they worked their way out from the inside. The machine was creating a creature.

The lights flickered like strobes and the screams stopped at the same time Johnny's breathing did. His body went limp in the chair.

"Bring him back … we're not done with him," a scientist yelled.

This is awful. As much as I hate Johnny for what he does to me, this isn't okay. I need to get up, to save him. Shouldn't I?

One of the men undid the straps from Johnny. Immediately, his lifeless body collapsed to the ground. The man ripped the goggles off Johnny's eyes and quickly held something up to his nose. He was breathing again.

He was still alive.

The man got up and left Johnny on the floor as the elevator beeped again. Someone else was here. *Don't tell me another kid is about to be tortured. I can't watch that again.*

"How close were we?" the new man asked as the doors opened. His voice sounded very familiar.

His dress shoes clacked across the cement as he walked closer to the clear box and as the hand slowly retreated into the brain. Inching my eyes upwards, I could see the man's blue dress pants, then his hanging lab coat, then his face.

It was Ed.

I knew that creep couldn't be trusted. But how did he fool Mom?

"We had a hand … we're almost there … we'll get it," one of the men replied.

"We need a real easily scared kid," Ed said, looking at the brain, which was morphing back together. "That creature will be the most evil invention of all time … and we're almost there." Then Ed's creepy, crooked smile spread across his face. "Back to work."

All of the scientists walked to the elevator. One stopped to retrieve Johnny.

"Leave him," Ed scolded. "It'll make him even more scared for next time."

The man nodded, ran to the elevator, and left with the others. The door closed and the green elevator arrow pointed up.

I nearly collapsed, while Shelly rushed over to Johnny. She tried lifting him, as he struggled to breathe.

"Do you believe me now?" The Impaler asked me.

"Yes, I'm sorry. Let's go," I urged.

"Hopefully it's not too late. The coin is still destroying the lake."

"How much worse could it get?"

"Everything in the water will die. Then the coin will burrow through the bottom of the lake. From there, it could go anywhere. It could kill everything," The Impaler informed us. "Water is the strongest catalyst for the coin. Its powers are amplified by it—like electricity. The evil powers within the coin will mix with the water, creating a toxic combination. Then I'm sure these crazy scientists will use it to create whatever that thing was."

Shelly and I gasped. *What have I done?* I thought the lake would have stopped all of this. Instead, it had made it worse.

"Come quick … we must go now," The Impaler instructed as he pressed the button, releasing the automatic door.

"What about him?" Shelly asked, pointing at Johnny, who was still nearly unconscious.

I reached down and pulled him up. His eyes rolled in his head like a ball in a pinball machine. Sure, part of me wanted to leave him here. I wanted him to pay for all of the times he made me feel crappy about myself. He deserved a little revenge, but I just couldn't do that. That wasn't who I was.

I motioned for Shelly to help. She rushed over and grabbed one arm while I held onto his other one, we dragged him out of the room.

The three of us rushed back through the long hallway, dragging Johnny and unlocking the doors as they came. We had to get out of here quickly to save the lake, and before the scientists returned. They'd know that someone broke in when they found Johnny gone.

We reached the shoreline where Shelly had originally found me. I was quickly chilled by the cold rain and the fact that I was still shirtless.

It was so dark, minus the red light from the cane.

We set Johnny down in the grass and The Impaler slammed his cane into the shoreline. It reached further as we looked out onto the water, which bubbled and reacted to the coin's powers. A few more fish had surfaced, and it was only a matter of time before the rest of them would too.

"I will go after the coin," The Impaler said.

"This was my fault. Let me get it." What was I saying? *Please say no.* I didn't really think I could do it. I was trying to be brave, but I wasn't brave enough for this.

"No. Only I can get the coin now. It was because of me that it was created, so I will have to find it. Besides, you cannot enter the water, your wound from the coin is too intense. It will scar you for life. You don't want to end up looking like me. Besides that, the surge of pain as you hit the water could be deadly. But I do need help," The Impaler looked at Shelly.

"I'm ready," Shelly said as she stepped forward, listening for her instructions. She didn't seem fazed, but I was freaking out inside. How would I ever explain this to my mom if something happened? Tell her that some scary kid made Shelly jump into the lake? Yeah right, she'd kill me. I couldn't. I wouldn't.

"No, I can't let her do—" I started to say, but I was interrupted.

"I've got this. You worry too much." Shelly patted my shoulder.

I groaned, hoping that she would be okay, but I needed to know what was about to happen. And so he explained. The Impaler needed Shelly to dive in after he retrieved the coin. He would signal for her, that way she wouldn't be exposed to the contaminated water for a long period of time. According to The Impaler, a human could only survive two minutes once the water was completely contaminated by the coin.

"Two minutes," he emphasized. "If it's any longer than that, you will die."

"Die?" I interjected. "No, I can't—"

The Impaler glared at me.

"I can't let—" I said, but before I could finish, Shelly covered my mouth. Then she nodded to The Impaler and repeated, "Two minutes."

"What about you?" Shelly asked The Impaler.

"Yeah, aren't you afraid of drowning?" I added.

"Don't worry about me," he replied.

Shelly listened to him and readied herself. I, on the other hand, was about to have a nervous breakdown. I set my watch to time them because I was going to be on pins and needles until she got out of the water.

"You will need to protect the coin," The Impaler said to me. He reached into his back pocket and pulled out a platinum case with a clear circular viewer in the middle. "This is the container I will put the coin into. It *must* stay there. Forever. Someone will come after the coin. You must prevent anyone from getting control of its powers. Otherwise, you and your family will be subject to the evils of the coin—all of its misfortune, plague, and death. You must protect the case. That is *your* job."

I reached out to shake his hand and thank him. Electricity shot through my body when our hands touched. "That's what it'll feel like if the evil powers like the ones inside the coin are ever used again. You've been touched by it like me, so you'll always know," The Impaler said. Shelly gave him a quick hug. A slight smile creased his face.

How was I so wrong about The Impaler? He was just a boy who had been experimented on by bad people. I thought *he* was bad, but he wasn't. He wanted to prevent the evil from getting out of the house and harming others.

"How will we know it worked?" I asked.

"Look for the light," he said, then darted toward the water.

"Wait!" I yelled. He turned back and looked at me.

"We don't know your name," I said.

"Wally Swanson."

He dove into the water.

Shelly and I looked at each other as goosebumps shot up my spine. Simultaneously, we mouthed "Swanson" to each other.

CHAPTER SIXTEEN

The red eyes glowed enough for us to see the outline of Wally. But as he got further away, his body shined neon green, like the color of the coin. It helped us track him as he went after the coin. Still, I wondered how he'd signal us when it was time for Shelly to dive in.

"Are you sure you're ready for this?" I asked, putting my arm around her.

Shelly was full of confidence. "I was born ready."

We both stared at the dangerous, red water. It was crazy to think that this was my doing, even crazier to think that it could have been worse. I was proud of Shelly, but upset with myself for letting her do this. "I can do it, you know."

"The Impaler—I mean, Wally, said you couldn't. I trust him," she said.

He'd proven himself and everything he'd said up to that point. *Why would he lie now?* We could have left, but this was bigger than us. We had to save our town and stop this coin from spreading its damage anywhere else.

I paced back and forth on the shore. I looked out, still waiting for Wally to summon Shelly. Nothing different yet. Then, I heard a strange noise. The lake started to ripple, the current dragged through it faster, and another fish shot to the surface. Then another. Then another. The coin was unleashing its evil on the water.

Out in the distance, a stream of light shot up from the lake. It grew brighter and higher until it looked like it reached the moon. Then Wally's head popped out of the water, followed by his hand holding the green, glowing coin. He quickly shoved the coin into the case. It was ready for Shelly.

She knew it was time. She looked at me and said, "See you in two."

Before Shelly could dive in, I grabbed her, pulled her in tight, and hugged her. She hugged back then quickly pushed me away to jump into the lake.

I started the timer on my watch, then looked out helplessly. Because of that stupid tree crashing down and the coin branding my chest,

I'd put my sister in danger. All I could do was hope that she'd be okay.

Shelly was moving quickly through the choppy water. She dodged dead fish that kept popping up in her way. She screamed when the first one came up, as it nearly crashed into her, but then it looked like she got used to the difficult conditions.

She was closing in on Wally. A few strokes more, then she reached out and grabbed the case from him.

He, and the light, disappeared back into the lake.

"I got it!" Shelly yelled. She caught her breath and started back to shore. I hoped the way back was as easy as the way out. But I was still worried. I couldn't stop thinking about Dad. I didn't want Shelly to disappear like he did.

The lake was fighting hard against Shelly. The furious water had embraced the coin's evil, and she was trying to stop it. The lake seemed to know that once the coin was removed, everything would return to normal. Maybe … it didn't want the evil to leave. Was something like this how Dad disappeared in the lake? Was it infected—haunted?

The water churned chaotic. Shelly's face popped up then went back under. She was far away, but I could see that the fight was taking its toll on her. She slowed down as she spat out water and struggled to breathe. I was frantic. Should I go in after her? Would we make it out alive if I did? What if Wally was wrong and it wouldn't affect me?

I had to try. I couldn't let my sister drown. Then none of us would survive and all that we'd done would be for nothing. I looked at my watch: 1:05. She only had fifty-five seconds left, or she could die from the toxic lake.

I ripped off my sneakers and jogged to the water. I kept looking for her, hoping that she'd show herself. But I still didn't see her. I got closer to the ripples. Another step, then the water touched my foot and splashed up my shin. It felt like I had been lit on fire! Pain scorched my leg and ran up into my chest. I couldn't go any further. I jumped back and fell to the ground. The pain was brief, but Wally was right. I'd been compromised by the coin.

Thirty-five seconds left, and I still couldn't see Shelly.

"Shelly ... Shelly. You can do it!" I screamed, but there was no response. "Please," I said to myself.

Thirty, twenty-nine, twenty-eight ...

I held the lantern higher. There was still no sign of her. The lake was extremely rough, and it continued to change color. It was the brightest shade of red I'd ever seen.

Twenty-five seconds …

I yelled and yelled.

Finally, her head shot out of the water. She was floating on her back, fighting for her life.

"Help, RJ!" she yelled in between swallowing mouthfuls of water.

Without thinking, I dove in. I had to. She was going to die.

The moment I hit the water, shooting pains electrified my body. I tensed up as numbing sensations rushed up my legs, into my arms, and my face. Then the pain spread and attacked my chest and my heart. Instantly, I felt every sore that was on my body come back.

My body locked up. *Ignore the pain, fight through it.*

I closed my eyes and swam, flapping my arms and kicking my feet as hard as I could. I wished that I had the coin in my possession now because then I'd be able to get through this lake without a problem. I felt a pull.

Something was pulling me back, preventing me from swimming faster. I lifted my head out of the lake, realizing that my hat was holding me back. There wasn't time for even the slightest drag, I had to get to Shelly immediately, so I ripped my hat off and threw it away from me. Saving Shelly was much more important than Dad's hat—even if it was the only thing I had left of him. He would've done the same.

I dove back under the water and kept my arm out, reaching until I felt something. I tried not to think about anything other than Shelly. Then I heard her voice.

My head shot out of the water and I saw her. Shelly was stuck, caught on the branch of a submerged tree, and couldn't get free. She was panicking and gasping for air. She was also running out of time.

I quickly glanced at my watch: fourteen seconds left.

There was no way that I'd be able to get her out of here in time, but I had to try.

I pulled at her pant leg, which was caught on the branch. I pulled harder. I couldn't get her unstuck. She reached down for me, and I surfaced. "Go RJ, take the coin. Get it out of here. Leave me."

I grabbed the case from her hand, stuffed it into my cargo pocket and made sure it was safe in there. Shelly looked so scared. It was awful to see. I wasn't going to leave her there. I dove back down under the water and used every bit of my strength to pull at her jeans. The denim started to rip. I had it. I tore the pants enough to free her leg and grabbed her hand.

I dragged her through the water, until we were a couple of feet from shore. *Beep, beep, beep* ... the two minutes had passed.

CHAPTER SEVENTEEN

I pulled Shelly onto the muddy shore. She was completely out of the water, and so was the coin, but nothing was changing, and she wasn't moving. Her body was lifeless.

"NO!" I yelled at the top of my lungs. What was I supposed to do? I struggled to think. I felt helpless. How could I have let her do this? Then I thought, *CPR class.*

I pressed hard against her sternum, trying to bring her back to life. "Come on, Shell," I begged.

I couldn't lose my sister. Not like this. Why did I throw the coin in the lake? What was it about this water that hated my family? This was all my fault.

I screamed and felt adrenaline rush through my veins. I pressed harder and harder against her sternum, time after time. Suddenly she spat water into my face and coughed violently.

"You're okay!" I grabbed Shelly and hugged her tightly.

Shelly shook me off, leaned on her side, and spat out what looked like blood, but it was the red lake water. "You saved me," she said, looking at me with a face full of fright. "But look at you. You're covered in those marks, just like Wally. Why did you—?"

"It doesn't matter," I said, glad that she was okay.

Thunder roared and lightning lit up the dark sky, which had now changed to an orange color. The wind whipped, and the waves swirled. The water shot into the sky, thousands of feet high, forming a tornado of water over the area where the lake once was.

This was magical, like nothing I'd ever seen before. We were able to see the empty dirt lakebed and the tree that nearly killed Shelly. The dead fish were scooped up into the tornado of water. We were mesmerized, but the winds were getting stronger and we were being sucked in.

I looked over to where we left Johnny to make sure he was still safe, but he was being sucked up into this whirlwind of water, too. I tried to reach for him, but it was too late. Shelly and I had to grab anything we could. We found a tree along the edge of the shoreline and hung on for dear life.

Suddenly, the tornado calmed. The water fell quickly towards the lakebed, changing back to a bluish color. Water slammed into the dirt bed and flooded the whole area. A tsunami-like wave hit hard and surged towards Shelly and me. We were finished—there was nowhere to go. That was all I remembered.

*   *   *

The sound of someone downstairs woke me. I sat up in my bed and looked around, wondering how I'd gotten home. I ripped the sheets off of my legs and jumped out of bed. I looked at my body—no sores. *Yes! I was healed.* I ran down the hallway to Shelly's room. She was sleeping in her bed, too.

Was this all a dream? I wondered. Then I heard the first of many rattles from the container that Wally had given us when he instructed me to keep watch over the coin. I went back into my room, following the sound. I dug through my pockets and found the coin all packaged in the platinum case. The coin flickered green through the clear circle in the middle of the case.

From behind, someone tapped my shoulder. I jumped. It was Shelly. Dang, she got me again.

"It was real, wasn't it?" I asked.

Shelly smiled. "Yeah, it was."

I felt an itchy, insect bite-like sensation on my chest. I lifted my shirt and the skull from the coin was etched into my skin again — it was the only mark I had left on me. Was it because I went into the water after Shelly?

We heard Mom downstairs. I pulled my shirt back down as Shelly and I ran down to see Mom. We stopped her as she walked through the kitchen, coffee mug in hand.

"Hey guys. You were both sound asleep when I got home. How was your night?" Mom asked while sipping her coffee.

"The best!" Shelly said, smirking at me.

"Where's Ed?" I asked. "Is he gone?"

"He'll be away for a little while. He has a big project he's working on," Mom said, sitting down at the table.

"Where?" I needed to know more about him and his work.

"The children's hospital that I work at. So I'll still be able to see him, but he probably won't be around here much," Mom said, sounding proud of Ed's work, "unless you guys want to volunteer to work with him."

Shelly and I looked at each other in fear. I bet my eyes were as big as hers.

Later that day, after we had an early dinner as a family, Shelly and I walked around the neighborhood. It wasn't as scary when it wasn't dark out.

We ended up back at thirteen—the old not-so-abandoned house. We snuck inside the creaky gate and walked around the property, staying out of the scientist's sight, in case they were still there.

It was mysterious and tough to explain, but I could feel Wally's presence.

Shelly and I wandered around the back of the castle to the cliff and looked down at the lake. It was bright blue, and fish were jumping out of the water. That time they went back underwater and kept swimming.

Who would've thought I'd be back here again? My mind wandered, thinking about Johnny. I hoped that everything went back to normal and he got out of the water tornado. I hoped he wasn't trapped in that house anymore, or worse.

I pulled out the platinum case and looked at the coin through the clear circle. This wasn't as scary as it had been the night before.

Everything was calm and peaceful and the view was beautiful from up there. It was even more amazing than I thought it would be, even though I still hated the lake for taking my father.

We kept walking the grounds until we saw the laundry chute that led to the flat burial ground. Next to it were some leaves that had been scattered across the ground covering something. I walked over to it—there was a ladder.

"Are you kidding me?" I called out.

Shelly laughed. "How did you miss that?"

I shook my head and pointed at the chute. "Wanna give it a try? You never got to last night!" I joked with Shelly.

"I guess since we can climb the ladder back up, why not?" Shelly shot through the tunnel, cheering with excitement. Then she hit the ground with a loud thud as she flew out of the slide.

"RJ, quick, you have to see this," Shelly yelled.

"I'm good. I already did that." I was completely against the idea of going through that tunnel again. It wasn't as scary tonight, but still, I was okay with never going down it again.

"Come here!" She yelled again with more urgency.

I groaned. "Really? You better not be messing with me."

"I'm serious, hurry up," she yelled back.

Against my better judgment, I gave in, but this time I took the ladder down. When I got to the ground, Shelly was there pointing at one of the many headstones that I didn't look at last night.

The first thing that I saw was my yellow bucket hat. My dad's hat. It was resting in front of a grave marker. I walked over to it and read the name on the stone. "Wally Swanson, 1980-1992. 12 trials."

He was already dead.

He'd given my hat back. I picked it up and put it on. I couldn't stop myself from smirking. So many thoughts filled my mind about Wally. If he was a ghost, how had I seen him? Would he ever be back again?

A bright light shot from the bottom of the lake to the moon. Shelly jumped back, but I barely flinched. Looking in my direction, she said, "Maybe you're not such a scaredy-cat after all."

We both looked out in awe, hoping that it was Wally.

Farther in the grass was a pair of VR goggles, much like the ones that were on Johnny, when he was hooked up to the brain. I was drawn to them.

My legs walked toward them as if they were magnetized. Before long, I was standing over the goggles. I couldn't stop myself from picking them up. Then I put them on top of my head, resting them there, but not yet looking through them.

"Are you gonna look?" Shelly asked, sneaking up from behind me.

I just looked at her, but didn't respond. I leaned my neck left, then right, cracking it slightly. Then reaching up for the goggles, I pulled them down and covered my eyes.

"Aughhhh! Snakes! Spiders! They're everywhere!" I screamed, ripping the goggles from my face. They couldn't stay there for another second. I was panting. My heart raced.

Bright spotlights erupted in the backyard. Then the doors to the house flew open and men rushed after us. We had nowhere to go.

I shook violently. Electricity flooded through me. *Oh no, is this what Wally was talking about? Is someone using the coin or some other version of its evil powers?*

The pain was blinding me—like I was about to pass out. I couldn't see the tombstone, goggles, or Shelly anymore. Everything was going blank. I shook my head like an *etch-a-sketch*, trying to clear my mind. But it didn't work.

My eyelids felt like thousands of pounds were hanging from them. I did everything I could to keep them open, but I couldn't fight any longer. My eyes shut.

I didn't know how much time passed, but my eyelids ripped open and I gasped for air. My head bobbed up and down as I looked around a dimly lit room. I wasn't able to move around very well. Then I heard voices from down the hall. One of them sounded like Ed's.

"Where is the subject?" an older man's voice asked, coming from somewhere outside of the room. I tried to pick my head up, but I couldn't. I was lying on my back on a hard bed. Where was I?

"He's being prepped for the nightmare room," another voice said, the one that sounded like Ed's.

"Have you built his nightmare yet—based on *all* of his fears?"

Build a nightmare? Was this for real? Was I about to go downstairs? I shifted my body, trying to sit up. I tried to lift my hand to wipe my eyes, but I couldn't. Both of them were restrained by straps with metal buckles.

Oh no. I panicked. The lights brightened as if they were fueled by my fright.

I tried to lift my legs, but they were also strapped down. Where was I? What was happening? *How long have I been here? Am I just like Wally—one of the kids that had been experimented on? Was I dead already too?*

I heard a deadbolt release. Someone entered the room and carefully closed the door behind them. Sweat bubbled under my armpit. My legs shook against the table. What was I supposed to do?

"RJ, finally I found you. Quick, we have to get out of here," Shelly's familiar voice came from inside the room, but I couldn't see her. Was she trapped too?

I felt hands on my arm—they were Shelly's! She quickly released the metal straps that held me and reached out to help me off the bed. I hopped down, but when I landed on the ground my lower back ignited on fire. I looked back to see what was causing it and I saw the imprint: "1890."

No. I was a patient? How long had I been there?

The vent in the corner of the room slid open and Wally squeezed through. "Let's go, RJ, now!" He yelled as the cell door started to slide open again.

"Grab the goggles," he said, pointing to the VR goggles that were on the counter near where I was held captive.

"For what?"

"You'll need them to get back here."

"Grab them, RJ!" Shelly yelled.

"I'm never coming back here," I yelled, refusing to grab them.

"You need them to save your dad. He's alive and can help stop all of this," Wally said as he disappeared back into the vent.

Dad? He's alive?

I didn't have any time. The door slid open. I could hear Ed's voice on the outside, "Oh RJ, it's about time we had that talk."

We had to get out of here otherwise I was headed to the nightmare room, and Shelly, too.

Shelly dove through the vent, then I went after her. We were safe, for now anyway. But I worried that the nightmare had just begun.

Check out a preview of the
next book in the

FRIGHTVISION

series:

Picture Day

(Featuring the nightmares of Julia Dove)

CHAPTER ONE

Picture day has always been especially challenging for me. I'm not a bad looking kid. I just think that I've had a run of particularly bad luck when it comes to me having my picture taken in front of a blue screen in the middle of the school gym.

There was the year I had something stuck in my teeth and no one told me. Then there was the year that I fell in the mud on the way to school. And who could ever forget the photographer that snapped my picture mid-sneeze? But, things got shockingly worse three years ago when my dentists convinced my parents that I needed braces … right before picture day.

When the teacher called everyone to get in line from shortest to tallest, I took my place in line behind the amazing Ruby Mitchel. She was perhaps an inch and a half shorter than I was with her hair in an avalanche of micro-braids pulled into a ponytail. As we made our way from the classroom and up the hall of Brockville Middle School towards the school gym, I watched the back and forth tick-tock pendulum of Ruby's braids and tried not to think about the mounds of wire and metal that encased my teeth. This would be the first year that Ruby Mitchel and I would stand together in our class photo. I was nervous because she was the prettiest and also the coolest girl in eighth grade.

I played her in several online gaming worlds and was always glad to have her bravery on my team whenever I could. She'd complimented me from time-to-time on my role-playing game skills, but I was certain that she wouldn't be interested in an awkward square like me with braces that seemed bigger than my mouth.

She walked from the line to the seat in front of the photographer, a tall slim man with pale skin and tiny, pointy teeth. She took a moment to swipe her braids behind her shoulders and straightened a crease in her powder blue dress. As she flashed a bright white smile towards the camera, I couldn't help thinking about how perfect she was. She stayed perfectly composed as the photographer counted down from three.

Then came the flash, and it was my turn to take the seat in front of the camera.

Reaching up to my face, I placed a hand on my mouth which was stretched farther than usual. I parted my lips, adjusting my jaw to the pressure. Suddenly, I felt the braces on my teeth grow outwards and then upwards covering nearly half of my face. I sat helplessly as the wires on my braces took on a life of their own and my heart sank as the photographer started his countdown.

"Wait," I tried to say, but the word was muffled in my attempt to talk with a mouth overflowing with brackets and wires. I looked to Ruby who was suddenly decked out in gamer battle gear, aiming her weapon towards the wayward wires.

"I gotcha, buddy," she said in the same voice she used when ready to assist in an online game attack.

"Say cheese," the photographer said with a maniacally strange accent that I couldn't quite place.

I wanted to tell him to wait again, but I was unable to respond. Ruby pointed her weapon as the flash of the bulb took me by surprise, blinding my eyes and sending me falling backwards. I bolted upright in bed.

My heart was racing a hundred miles a minute as I reached up to my mouth to feel perfectly straightened teeth with no braces. I took in a deep breath and exhaled, laughing slightly at the silliness of the bad dream about a picture day that had seemed to be so real. Seconds later, the alarm on my cell phone rang. It was time for me to get up for school.

I hopped from my bed and hurried to shower and get dressed. It was indeed picture day. I would be able to stand next to Ruby in our class photo and would no longer have to smile through brackets and wires. To top it off, Mom had taken me to the mall the prior weekend for new clothes and a special haircut. I didn't mind seeing my bushy black curls chopped down to the faded, side-swept faux hawk I'd chosen from a magazine. After brushing my teeth, I pushed the sides of my hair down and combed the top up and to one side like the barber had shown me.

I felt like a new man. New clothes, smooth brown acne-free complexion, and bright white smile. I really hoped that Ruby would notice. Frowning just a little, I picked up my retainer case. Opening it, I popped the retainer in my mouth, reminding myself that I could take it out right before the photo. I grabbed a jacket and book bag, rushing past the kitchen with the delicious aroma of breakfast wafting through the hall. I didn't want to get any food stuck between my teeth again. Not before pictures.

"Eli, are you hungry?" Mom called as I reached the door.

"No!"

She exited the kitchen just in time to see me open the door. "Elias Green, you know I am not going to let you out of this house without breakfast."

"It's picture day, Mom!"

She nodded. "Well, at least drink a little milk and take a breakfast bar in case you get hungry." She waited for me to drink the milk down and put the breakfast bar in the side pocket on my book bag.

"You are so handsome." She reached out to tussle my hair, but I dodged it before she could.

"Picture day," I reminded her again.

I escaped the house, hopped on my bike and peddled from the driveway to the sidewalk, where my best friend Tim was waiting for me at the corner. Tim looked the same as he did every day, with his blonde hair cropped close to his head, almost military style, and wire rimmed glasses in front of his brown eyes. He was casually flipping through the latest issue of whatever his newest comic book series was, until he saw me.

"Whoa!"

"I know, right?"

"That's a good look on you, bro." He hurried the comic into his book bag and then gave me a fist bump.

"You think Ruby will like it?"

"I guess we are about to find out. You gonna ask her to the dance?"

"I think so."

We biked through the neighborhood until we reached the school. Groups of kids clumped together were taking selfies in front of the school. I wasn't the only one that put in extra effort for picture day. Tim and I met up with other bikers at the bike rack, locking into the usual place. Kids loved my haircut and even a few girls asked to take selfies with me before going into school. And then, there she was. Ruby rounded the corner. She was too pretty for words. She wore a dark blue sweater that fit snug over her powder blue dress. Her braids were pulled up into a bun that was nearly the size of her cinnamon brown face. As she approached it was hard to speak.

"Hey Eli, great haircut."

"Thanks." I felt heat rise in my cheeks.

"You wanna take a selfie with us?" Tim stepped in for me.

"Of course," she said. The three of us goofed around in front of Tim's camera phone until the first bell rang. In several shots, Ruby put her arm around my shoulder, then my waist, and she even hugged me. For the first time in my life, as we walked into the school together, I felt popular and cool.

CHAPTER TWO

We filed into the school and my class was directed to go straight to the gym. We left our jackets and bags on the bleachers and Ms. Vada, our homeroom teacher, quickly ushered us from the bleachers to our place in line for our class photo. I took the time to take one last look at myself in my camera phone.

"You look marvelous, darling!" the photographer marched up and down the line as he inspected our outfits and hair. "Alright children." His accent reminded me a little bit of the accent from old vampire movies and, as my imagination began to run away with me, I wondered if maybe his skin was a little too pale and his K-9s were a little too sharp. Then I remembered the photographer from my dream. It couldn't be. I couldn't have dreamed of this particular photographer. "I am Monsieur Laurent. You all look absolutely lovely and it is my great pleasure to capture you today."

It was a strange introduction, one that I had never gotten from a school photographer and one that sent a creepy chill up my back. I shook off the sensation, deciding that my imagination was simply working overtime. When it came time for our class to get on the risers in front of a cloud screen and lights, Ms. Vada lined us up from shortest to tallest and, just like in my dream; Ruby stood right in front of me. Tim, being one of the tallest kids in our class, stood towards the back. Seeing that I was standing right beside Ruby, he gave me a thumbs up and I flashed him a triumphant smile.

And right then, in that moment, I realized that I'd forgotten to take out my retainer. The students were filing onto the risers one by one. Should I keep the retainer in or take it out? I was stuck in the very center of the middle row, so slowly I lifted my hand to reach for the retainer. Just then, Ruby reached for my fingers and held my hand. I felt my entire face fall in shock. I looked at her to be sure that she knew that it was my hand she held. She turned to me with a little smile, her large brown eyes twinkling. Forgetting my retainer, I smiled.

"Everyone look up here," Monsieur Laurent called to the class. "All eyes please," he repeated as he waited for someone to follow instructions. "Tres bien," he said. I relaxed a bit as I was able to finally place his accent. French. "Good children! Everyone, look directly into the camera and I will count down."

I kept my face angled towards the camera, gripping Ruby's hand and broadening my smile into what I was sure was the goofiest grin of anyone in the history of middle school class pictures.

"Un, deux, trois," he counted. "Say, fromage!" Monsieur Laurent called.

"Fromage!" the entire class repeated and the flash of the bulb hit all of us.

Blue stars blinded me for a moment, until I felt ushered down the risers by the movement of the class. Ruby loosened her grip on my hand and reluctantly, I let go. The soft warmth of her grasp lingered on my palm as we lined up once again from shortest to tallest. Why had she held my hand? What did that mean? Did she like me the way I liked her? Would she say yes if I asked her to the dance on Friday? As she took her turn in front of the camera, right before she was to smile and say "Fromage," she winked at me.

Next, it was my turn.

"Now, look directly into the camera, Monsieur Green, and say fromage."

Not even wondering how on earth this photographer new my last name, I ran my tongue over the slim wire of my retainer. The only fact I cared about was that Ruby had held my hand and then winked at me. I repeated the word "fromage" with a huge, goofy grin. I cannot really describe what happened next other than to say that once the bulbs flashed I felt a lightning bolt sensation strike my retainer, buzzing over my teeth and through my mouth.

"Youch!" I fell backwards from the chair, my back slamming into the floor. The fall knocked all of the wind out of my lungs and it took several moments before I could regain my breath and sit up.

"Are you alright?" He hurried from his place behind the camera to help me back up on my feet.

"Yeah, I'm fine." I brushed off my clothes and ran my hand over my hair. "Can I take another one?"

"Sorry kid, one take per student."

"Are you serious?" I asked. "There is no way that picture will come out alright."

"Thems the breaks." He chucked me on the shoulder and ushered the next student into the chair.

I took my seat on the bleachers next to Ruby and we waited with the rest of the class for everyone else to finish.

"He wouldn't let you take another picture?"

"No," I said, pouting.

"What happened?" Ruby asked. "One minute you were smiling in the chair and the next you were falling to the floor with smoke coming from your mouth!"

"Smoke?" I asked in surprise.

"Yeah, and I could have sworn there was electricity in your mouth."

"Well, it certainly felt like a shock of some kind." I ran my tongue over my teeth and the retainer wire to see if anything felt different. Taking my phone from my pocket I flashed a smile for the camera, then opened wide to see if I could see any damages. There was nothing.

"That was weird." Tim added as he sat down with us. "What happened?"

"We're trying to figure that out. It looked like there was some sort of electrical shock in his mouth," Ruby explained.

"Cool!" Tim adjusted his glasses and leaned in closer to take a look at my teeth. "That's like the stuff that happens just before people turn into superheroes ... or mutants."

"Get real," Ruby said.

"I'm serious!" Tim continued, "Every time a superhero or mutant is born, or their long dormant powers emerge ... it happens like right after a freaky accident of some kind."

Tim sat back and began looking me over from head to toe.

"What are you doing?" I felt uncomfortable under his scrutiny.

"Well, when mutations or powers emerge, sometimes they also come with deformities," he explained.

"I'm not deformed!"

"Well, no. Not yet. But keep an eye out for bubbling flesh that begins to grow or ..." he hesitated a moment.

"Or what?" I asked, hooked on his every word and wanting to know what else I should look out for besides bubbling flesh.

"Or growing extra limbs," Tim concluded.

"That's ridiculous," Ruby chimed in, but I began to imagine my own body covered in bubbling flesh and growing extra arms and legs.

"Yeah," Tim conceded. "That kind of weird and gross stuff only happens to bad guys that have an axe to grind and immediately use their powers and mutations to plot revenge. There is no way that Eli would ever be a bad guy. So, no worries, buddy. You get to keep your pretty human form."

I couldn't find any words to respond to Tim's scenario.

"You've been reading way too many comics," Ruby jumped in.

It was dawning on me that my dream from the night before about picture day had been eerily similar.

"Alright, class," Ms. Vada called when pictures were finished. "Let's get to homeroom and start our day with some U.S. History."

"Or herstory," Ruby muttered, getting in line next to me once again.

"Are you alright, Eli?" Ms. Vada asked. "You took quite a tumble. Do you want to go see the school nurse?"

"No, I'm great," I assured her, but what I was really thinking about was Ruby holding my hand and winking at me as we marched through the hallway to class. We made a stop by our lockers to put away our jackets and cell phones and to get the books we needed for class.

I felt as if I was walking on air as Ruby waited for me by the door. Despite what had happened in the gym, maybe now would be the best time to ask Ruby to the dance. I was slowly building up my confidence. However, that kind of shattered when I walked into the classroom and straight into Carter Wilson's fist.